Dreaming

of Horses

Ag
argenta
press

Mary Razzell

© 2013 Mary Razzell
First printed in 2013 10 9 8 7 6 5 4 3 2 1
Printed in Canada

All rights reserved. No part of this work covered by the copyrights hereon may be reproduced or used in any form or by any means—graphic, electronic or mechanical—without the prior written permission of the publisher, except for reviewers, who may quote brief passages. Any request for photocopying, recording, taping or storage on information retrieval systems of any part of this work shall be directed in writing to the publisher.

The Publisher: Argenta Press (an imprint of Dragon Hill Publishing Ltd.)

Library and Archives Canada Cataloguing in Publication

Razzell, Mary, 1930–, author
        Dreaming of horses / Mary Razzell.

ISBN 978-1-896124-59-9 (pbk.)

        I. Title.

PS8585.A99D74 2013   C813'.54   C2013-903606-7

Project Director: Marina Michaelides
Project Editor: Gary Whyte
Cover Image: Front cover: girl laying in field © Aleshyn Andrei / Shutterstock; horses © Maria Itina / Photos.com; back cover: (modified from front cover image)
Title Page Image: Photo © Mary Razzell

Produced with the assistance of the Government of Alberta, Alberta Multimedia Development Fund.

PC: 1

Dedication

~

In loving memory of my husband
Eric Nicol
1919–2011

Acknowledgements

~

I am appreciative of our neighbours on the North Hill of Calgary in the 1930s. Without their good and kind hearts, my own mother would not have survived.

I remember with gratitude the late John Patrick Gillese, founding director of Alberta Culture's Film and Literary Arts Branch, who first encouraged me to write.

Special thanks to Gary Whyte whose editing made it the best book it could be.

CHAPTER
one

Lately I've started dreaming about horses again, great dark-eyed horses with sleek coats, hot and moist, under my hand and with breath live as yeast.

The first time I dreamed about horses was the September when I was seven. That was in Calgary, in 1937, the worst year of the Depression, historians now say. The neighbours murmured of "wind and dust," and anxiety tightened the corners of their eyes.

Kitty-corner from our house on the North Hill was a grocery store and right next door to it, a butcher shop. Behind them lay a courtyard of hard-packed earth with five horse stables clustered around it.

Three of the horses had been sold, and the remaining two were destined for the glue factory—or so said our next-door neighbour, Mrs. Bruce, who seemed to know everything going on in the neighbourhood. Her husband was a bank manager downtown and one of the few men on our street in those times who had a job.

The two horses were lethargic and gaunt-hipped, but they would hang their heads over the stall doors and nicker whenever I entered the courtyard. I was fascinated by their stiff eyelashes and wide, flaring nostrils, and I felt a tenderness towards them when their ears pricked up as I approached.

The courtyard was the unofficial meeting place of the older neighbourhood boys. My older brother Paul, who was thirteen, had ordered me to stay away. "If it was just me, it would be okay. But it's the other guys—they don't want girls hanging around, especially kid sisters."

But every morning after breakfast—and before the neighbourhood boys were out—I raced over to the courtyard to see if the horses were still there. Over the weeks that followed, I watched as their coats grew sparse, and their eyes lost their lustre.

I began to dream about the horses, and I always had the same dream. I would lead the horses to the wide open prairie that lay behind our house and let them go, my heart pounding to the rhythm of their hoofbeats as they wheeled away to the foothills, the floating shapes of the Rockies beyond.

One late Saturday afternoon that September, Paul and his friends were scrounging around the neighbourhood for old lumber for a bonfire. They soon had a pile of broken fence pickets, bashed-in apple boxes, and tree branches that had come down during the last wind. All were carted to the vacant lot next to the grocery store–butcher shop compound.

I went over to watch. Billy Bruce, the biggest of the boys, called to me. "Sheila, run over to your house and get us a couple of matches."

I squirmed and looked down. "My mother doesn't allow me to touch the matches," I said. Where was Paul? I always felt safer when he was nearby.

"But you know where they are, don't you?" Billy said. Now his frayed running shoes had planted themselves before me. "So get us a couple." His voice took on a coaxing quality. "Your mother wouldn't mind for something like this. Besides, if you get the matches, we'll roast a potato for you in our bonfire."

"I'm not allowed to stay out after dark," I said, looking up at him for the first time. "So I couldn't eat it anyway."

"Paul can take it home to you," said Billy. I hesitated as the image of a black, charred potato with steaming, white flesh grew more and more vivid in my mind.

Billy clamped a hand on my shoulder. "Come on," he said roughly. "Don't be such a baby."

"I'm not a baby! Why can't you get your own matches from your house?"

"Because I need to be here to make sure everything gets done. All I'm asking for is two matches." Then, softly, "Tell you what. I'll get the other guys to let you come and visit the horses anytime you want. You know those old nags aren't going to be around here much longer. This may be your last chance."

I looked over at the horses. They seemed to smile at me with their velvet lips.

I ran home across a street that was suspended in the yellow glow of the setting sun. Quietly I opened the back door. The kitchen and pantry were deserted. Sounds of my two younger brothers, Tom, five, and Andy, who was almost one, came from the living room. I heard the scrape of a chair and my mother's footsteps. Then the radio was turned on with a spate of static, and an organ began to play the theme music for *The Lux Radio Theatre*.

I knew that the wooden matches were stored in a jar on the top shelf of the pantry. I climbed up on the counter and reached for it. The lid was hard to unscrew, and the jar held only six matches. My fingers closed on two of them. I stared at their blue heads tipped with red. The matches felt alive in my trembling hand.

As I began to move stealthily towards the back door, my mother's voice called from the living room. "Is that you, Sheila?"

I stopped, hand on the doorknob. "Yes, Mom." Something seemed stuck at the back of my throat.

"What are you up to?"

"Just getting a drink of water." I ran the tap and filled the tin drinking-cup that sat on the wooden drain board. But I couldn't swallow, and the water ran down my chin. Leaving the cup in the sink, I bolted out the back door to the vacant lot and Billy Bruce.

The light was beginning to fade, and the boys looked like black silhouettes against the dying sunset. Suddenly, Billy stood in front of me. He smelled musty, like earth and leaves and worms. Wordlessly, I handed over the two matches.

I stayed just long enough to see the fire catch, the flames dart up, blue and red, into the purple dusk. The sky looked heavy and sullen, and the air felt colder, too, with a smell of snow in it. A strong wind gusted from the northeast and rattled the tree branches. I shivered.

As I crossed the street back home, I heard the horses neigh from their stalls. I could feel their great, dark eyes following me.

By the time we were ready to go to bed that night, the wind had increased. "I wouldn't be at all surprised if we had a blizzard by dawn," my mother said. "I hope your father won't try and drive in this weather." Dad was due back from Edmonton where he had gone to look for a job. Worry lines webbed her forehead.

I slept on the chesterfield in the living room. My three brothers slept in one of the bedrooms, my parents in the other. Sometime during the night, I became conscious of the wail of fire sirens. Half-asleep, I groped my way to the front window.

Flames shot up in the darkness from the direction of the stables. As I watched, one of the supporting timbers gave way, and a crescendo of sparks exploded high against the black sky. I heard a high-pitched whinny of fear, and a jolt went through me. My scalp prickled, and for a moment, I thought I was going to drop, but my forehead came to rest against the cold windowpane, and my head cleared.

With my heart banging against my ribs, I watched the firemen drag hoses from their truck. Steam rose where the water hit the flames. It seemed like hours before they got the fire out. By this time, my whole family was standing around the front window. I moved to stand close to Paul for comfort. As a faint stench of charred flesh seeped into the house, saliva flooded my mouth, and I made it just in time to kneel in front of the open toilet bowl.

My mother came in later and found me still on my knees and shivering. "You poor child. And you're cold, too," she murmured, taking off her sweater and draping it around my shoulders as she led me back to bed.

~

I woke in the morning, hoping it had all been a nightmare. Rushing to the front window, I pushed back the worn lace curtain. Snow was blowing almost horizontally, but in spite of the swirling flakes, I could see the blackened stumps of what used to be the stables. The flat, dead smell of ashes came in through the three air holes at the bottom of the wooden window frame.

I was whimpering inside as I pulled on my clothes and went into the kitchen. Mom was bringing in the milk from the back porch, the cream frozen and sitting above the tops of the bottles like cocked hats.

"Mrs. Bruce has been in already this morning to visit," Mom said, putting the milk away in the pantry. "That woman must get up at the crack of dawn. Whatever for, I'll never know. There's not enough work in that house to keep her busy. With just the one child, and all the modern conveniences she has—"

I broke in. "What about the fire? The horses?"

"Both horses were burned to death." She began to add oatmeal to the pot of water on the stove. "There's to be an investigation by the fire marshal later this morning."

"Investigation?"

"To investigate the cause," Mom said impatiently. "People do set fires to collect insurance, you know." She paused long enough to turn down the gas flame. "Or the fire could have been set by someone who didn't like the horses. There are folks in this neighbourhood who said the horses didn't belong inside the city limits, probably the same ones who reported us for having a cow in the vacant field behind our house." Her face hardened, and her voice became indignant. "With all that empty prairie behind us going to waste! And me with all these hungry mouths to feed! Well, I'm not mentioning any names, but…." She tipped her head in the direction of the Bruces' house.

My teeth began to chatter. "Whatever is the matter with you?" Mom asked, placing a warm hand on my forehead. "Sick last night and now this. Don't tell me you're coming down with something, and Andy just over the croup."

All I could think of was the horses burning. Once more I saw the flames shooting skyward. In my mind's eye, I saw the horses rear back in terror, the red of the fire reflecting in their eyes.

"I've got to see for myself," I said, pulling away from Mom's hand.

"But you haven't even had your porridge—"

I didn't wait to hear the rest.

⁓

Several of the bigger boys were already at the courtyard, poking around the fallen timbers. But not my brother, Paul. Where was he?

The snow gusted around us until we all looked like ghosts. I saw the figure of an adult drifting towards us.

Through the whiteness came a gravelly voice. "You kids had a fire here last night, didn't you?" For one terrible moment, I thought it was God. But it was old Bill Green, the bachelor who lived in a tiny house in the middle of our block. As he got closer, I saw that his eyes were fierce beneath the peak of his cap. Scowling at me, he pulled the cap even lower over his fore-head. The ear flaps, untied, hung like bat wings.

"Well, isn't that so?" he demanded. "Speak up, girl. You've got plenty to say for yourself most other times."

I looked around wildly and saw that I was alone. The flee-ing shapes of the boys were fast disappearing through the slanting snow.

"Terrible thing this country's coming to. Young 'uns going around settin' fires wheresoever they take a notion. Burnin' up valuable livestock. If I was your father—which I ain't and glad of it, too—I'd take the strap to the whole lot of you. I guaran-tee none of you would sit down for a week."

I began to move backwards. I wanted to cry out that I hadn't set the fire, that it had been the bigger boys. Not Paul, but the others.

"I've got a good mind to speak to your folks," Mr. Green was saying, a large drop of moisture forming at the end of his rheumy nose.

I turned and ran. The snow stung my eyes as I slid and slipped through the blind, white world. I finally had to stop because of a stitch in my side.

Sounds of singing came muffled through the falling snow, and I saw that I was outside the United Church, which was at the far end of the block. I didn't want to go home, so I went inside.

"Holy, holy, holy!" sang the congregation. "Lord God Almighty! Early in the morning our song shall rise to Thee." I found an empty space in one of the back pews. Mr. Bruce—who was acting as usher—saw me, and a look of disbelief and then displeasure crossed his face. I looked down at my coat. It was buttoned unevenly, and part of the hem had come undone. All around me, people were wearing their Sunday best. I slid down in the pew trying to be less conspicuous.

The minister, a tired, dry-looking man, read from a huge bible. The reading was a seemingly endless account of plagues and of God hardening the heart of Pharaoh. By the time he'd read how the waters had receded for Moses but had covered and drowned the Egyptian horses, I was sitting on the edge of my seat, trembling with anger.

The offering-plate appeared before me attached to the end of Mr. Bruce's arm. I had nothing to give. Even if I had a penny, I wouldn't have put it on the green-felt lined plate. Not to support such cruelty as God had shown towards the Egyptian horses. I was shocked that everyone around me looked complacent, as if we hadn't just been read a horror story.

I wasn't feeling any better by the time the service ended. The sermon and the hymns had done nothing to lessen the guilt I felt about the horses that died in the fire. If anything, they made me feel worse.

Martha Beryl, my best friend, was outside the front door of the church as I left. She was with her grandmother. "Why, Sheila Brary," exclaimed Mrs. Beryl. "What a surprise! I thought your family was Catholic."

"Only when my dad's not home."

A slight spasm twitched the corner of Mrs. Beryl's mouth, as if she were trying not to smile. "Oh. Well, how did you enjoy the sermon?"

"I didn't," I answered.

"Oh, my," she said softly. Then, "Would you like to come home and have lunch with us? You could stop and ask your mother on the way if it's all right with her."

"It will be," I answered quickly. Mom didn't usually care where I was, especially if I stayed away for a meal. It meant that much more food for the rest of them.

I stayed away from home until late afternoon. By that time, the snow had stopped. I began to wonder if Dad had made it back from Edmonton.

But my father was not home. I knew that as soon as I opened the back door. The house still had that empty waiting feel to it. Disappointed, I hung up my coat.

Mom's voice from the living room was harsh. "Is that you, Sheila? You march right in here."

Mom's face looked like a storm was crossing it. "Where have you been?" she demanded.

"At Martha Beryl's."

Her eyes bored into mine. In a flat voice she asked, "Have you been at the matches, Sheila?"

I stopped breathing for a moment.

"There! Just as I thought!" she said triumphantly. "It's written all over your face. And just what did you do with the two matches you took? You think I don't know how many matches I had left?"

"The boys wanted them to start the bonfire yesterday."

"And all they had to do was ask you, and you would steal them from your own family." Her face flushed. "You always do for the outsider, just like your father. You know the fire was responsible for killing the horses. If you hadn't stolen those matches—like a common little thief—those two horses would be alive today."

"No, Mom!"

"A fine thing," she said, her voice rising, "you traipsing off to church this morning. Oh, yes, the neighbours couldn't wait to tell me all about it. 'Is your Sheila not going to the Catholic Church anymore?' they want to know. The very idea of a seven-year-old girl deciding a thing like that! Why you would want to be filling your head with all that heathenish pap from the Protestants…"

"Mom, I—"

"Those people are there for one thing and one thing only, and that is, who can butter their bread. Stand up straight when I'm talking to you."

I couldn't. The enormity of what she said, about me being responsible for the death of the horses, left me reeling, and I thought that I would crash to the floor. Half of me cried out that it couldn't be true. The other half whispered that it was.

I wished Dad were home. But he wasn't.

CHAPTER
two

Dad didn't come home that day. Or the next. A week passed, then two, and still no word from him. My mother looked more haggard each day as she tried to stretch the little money she had to keep us fed.

"I'll have to sell the piano to try and make ends meet," she said to Paul. "I'm sure I don't know what I'm going to do next. There's no one here I can talk to. If only I had some family in Canada, it wouldn't be so bad." Most of Mom's family was in Ireland, and she never let on to them the troubles we had. Increasingly, Mom was turning to Paul when she had a problem, even though he was only thirteen.

She cried the day she sold the piano. "I didn't learn to play until after I came to Canada in 1921," she said. She told us that she had to work for a family of nine in Regina to pay off the balance of her passage over from Ireland. "That's the way the Canadian immigration office did it," she said. "You paid them eight pounds as part of your fare to Canada, and you had two years without interest to pay back the balance. They promised you a job. The family I was sent to had a summer cottage at Long Lake. Water had to be carried, and I was told to change the dishwater only once a week. I said to the wife, 'Sure, it would be far better if we washed the dishes only once a week in clean water, rather than be putting our dishes in the likes of that.' In a few days, that water had a thick scum of grease on its surface. But she said, 'No, do it my way.' I left there to work in the dining room at St. Chad's School for Girls in Regina. I paid for music lessons, and the Anglican nuns let me practice on their piano."

"You could apply for relief, Mom," said Paul.

Mom shook her head. "Only as a last resort. Think of the shame of it! No, if I could get a job, do a bit of housework, the way I did for that doctor's wife in Elbow Park…. But no one wants a woman this far along."

This far along. Those were the words she had used when she had been expecting Andy. I looked at my mother closely and saw the swelling there under her loose-fitting housedress. "There's only one thing left to do," Mom fretted. "I'll take in boarders. I'll rent out the dining room. It's large and sunny and has a door for privacy, and there's that nice tree outside the window." Her voice became animated. "Yes, that's what I'll do. My crocheted bedspread. A bit of wax on the floor…clean curtains…. Do you children have any money for an ad in the paper? I'm down to our last dollar."

Paul gave her a quarter, all he had. I eased a kitchen knife into my piggy bank and slid out two lone pennies. Tom contributed a nickel.

The same afternoon that the ad appeared, a Mrs. Powers and her daughter Grace came knocking on our front door.

"We've come in by bus from Olds," she said. "My husband is here in the hospital with TB."

Mrs. Powers had a face like a fading rose. Her daughter was nine but in grade two, the same as me. Grace's eyes had a peculiar slant. Her face was full moon, and mucous from her nose chapped her lips.

"Grace is a little…well…behind in many ways," Mrs. Powers said. "She needs help with simple things, like being reminded to go to the bathroom."

"Our Sheila can help keep an eye on her," my mother volunteered.

"That would be such a help," Mrs. Powers said gratefully, her eyes shimmering with tears. "I'd like to spend as much time as I can at the hospital with Mr. Powers. The doctors are not very hopeful, I'm afraid."

Money and the front door key were exchanged.

In the days that followed, I was stuck with taking care of Grace. I did it ungraciously. But Mom looked less strained now that she had money coming in regularly and an adult to talk to in the evening. She still worried about Dad and why he hadn't written, and the last thing she did every evening was to go to the front window and look up and down the street, as if hoping to see his car. Then, with a sigh, she would let the lace curtain drop back and walk slowly to her bedroom.

Some of the talk between Mrs. Powers and Mom was about me. "She's like her father," I overheard Mom say. "I never have a moment's peace with her. Not like Tom. He's an angel. Do you know that two springs ago Sheila smashed in the front window, all in a fit of temper? It's not that I've spared the rod with her, either. I've taken the strap to her many a time, but she's got the devil in her."

This is what happened. A late March day with a Chinook warming the air. Water from the melted snow running in torrents along the street gutters. Martha and I take our dolls out onto the sidewalk, and when we tire of that, we go out to the foothills behind our street and search their southern slopes for wild crocuses. We find several clumps—they are like Easter eggs, pale white and yellow and mauve—and we pick handfuls to take home.

By the time we get back, I've left it almost too late to go to the bathroom, and the urge to do number one is strong. At that moment, a kitten comes meowing out from behind a bush, and Martha stops to pat it. Now I'm dancing from one foot to the other because I know I can't hold it any longer. When I get to our front door, Tom—who must have seen me coming—locks the door in my face. Frantic, I hammer on the door. "Let me in!" I shout.

"Go around to the back," Tom calls through the keyhole. "It's unlocked."

I run round to the back door just in time to hear him shoot the bolt across. "Tom," I wail, "I've got to go to the bathroom RIGHT NOW!"

"The front door's unlocked. Go try there."

My underwear pants are beginning to feel damp. I run around to the front door again, just in time to hear a smart click as the key is turned.

I ball up my fist and smash in the front window.
Tom unlocks the front door, his face white and his
eyes huge. My mother comes running to see what the
commotion is all about.

"I have to go to the bathroom, and Tom locked me
out. Both doors," I say between clenched teeth. I march
past both of them, so angry that I'm rigid.

When I finish in the bathroom, Mom has the strap
out. But by now I don't care, and I don't cry when she
uses it. Nor do I cry anytime of that long afternoon that
I'm banished to the boys' bedroom.

I refuse to talk to anyone about it. But, after that,
I make sure I never have to go to the bathroom that
badly again, even if it means squatting out in the hills
with the cold wind whistling around my bare bottom.

My teacher Miss Campbell announced that our grade two
class was to put on a Nativity play at the Christmas concert.
"This is really an honour," she said, the two spots of rouge on
her checks seeming to brighten with her enthusiasm. "We must
all work very hard to make it a success." She consulted a sheaf
of papers in her hand. "There are only five speaking parts in the
play, but you will all have a chance to participate in some way.
We'll need costumes. They can be made from fifteen cents
worth of cheesecloth, and I'm sure your mothers won't find
them too difficult to make. I'll send home a note with each of
you today with a description of the costume needed."

The class was absolutely still while Miss Campbell assigned
the parts. Martha Beryl was chosen to be an angel, and no

wonder. She would make a perfect angel with her long golden ringlets that her grandmother set with rags every night. I prayed that I'd get a part, one with lots of lines and plenty of time on stage. And not something ridiculous, please God, like being the back end of the donkey.

"Sheila Brary." At the sound of my name, I straightened up in my seat. "I've chosen you to be Mary, the mother of Jesus. There's a fair bit of memorizing to do, but I'm sure you'll be fine. Would you like to be Mary?"

Would I? "Yes, Miss Campbell."

She began to hand out the notes of instruction for our mothers on how to make the costumes. Mine read, "*Blackfoot Indian maiden. Use cheesecloth to make a simple dress, such as would have been made from deerskin. Headband can be made in class by pupil.*" I already had an idea for a geometric design for the headband, using red, violet and yellow-green. We had been doing complementary colour schemes in art, and I liked this colour combination best.

By lunchtime, I was so excited about the play that I ran all the way home. A Chinook wind had melted the snow, and water was swirling in the street gutters. Sparrows chirped in the bare bushes as I turned in at my home.

As soon as I opened the back door, I smelled macaroni and cheese, my favourite. The casserole sat on the opened oven door, all golden brown and with crunchy bits along the edge. Andy was already in his high chair drinking milk.

"Guess what, Mom?" I said, bursting with my news. "We're having a Christmas play, and Miss Campbell says I'm to be Mary, the Virgin Mother. She says that all you have to do is make the costume. She's sent home the instructions." I dug into my coat pocket and gave Mom the note. "Miss Campbell says it'll only cost fifteen cents for the cheesecloth. Martha's going to be—"

"Fifteen cents!" my mother exploded. "I could buy a pound-and-a-half of baloney for fifteen cents, enough to feed the seven of us for supper! No, it's out of the question." She thrust the note back at me, unread.

"But, Mom!" I stared at her, not believing that she couldn't see how important this was.

"I don't know what your teacher can be thinking of," she said abruptly, turning away. "It's a cinch she isn't trying to raise a family on next-to-nothing. Bad enough we're in a Depression and with a father like yours. No word from him. Two months now to the day. And Christmas coming. As if he cared!"

My stomach twisted. I hated it when she talked this way about my father.

"The mortgage is due," she went on, serving up the macaroni and cheese with a harsh clatter of spoon. "I have a tooth that needs pulled—I haven't been able to sleep all week with it. And Tom should have new boots. While here you are, wanting a fancy costume. You're just like your father, Sheila, always thinking of yourself."

"No, Mom!" I cried out. Then, "All the other kids will have costumes."

"Even if we did have the money—which we don't—I have no time to be making costumes." Mom slammed the plates on the table.

The kitchen that had seemed so warm and full of good smells looked ugly now. I saw the brown linoleum curling in the corners, its pattern faded in front of the sink and stove. The white enamelled table in front of me was chipped. Andy sat still, his eyes round like the ring of milk around his mouth. Tom moved his chair away from mine.

I began to eat. The macaroni and cheese stuck at the back of my throat. I choked.

The door opened. It was Grace, mucous from nose to lip, wet panties sagging below her dress. In my excitement of being chosen to be Mary, I'd forgotten all about her.

Mom looked at me over the bowl of jelly she was bringing in from the pantry. "You didn't wait for Grace, did you?" she accused. I concentrated on the dessert dishes, anything to avoid the anger in my mother's eyes. Cream-coloured, the dishes had an embossed pattern of nasturtiums and green vines trailing around the edges. We got them every Friday night from the Crescent, the neighbourhood movie theatre. For the admission price of ten cents, the Crescent showed a double feature and gave away a different piece of china each week.

"Sheila, do you hear me talking to you?" Mom's voice broke into my thoughts.

I couldn't meet her eyes. "Yes, Mom."

"You're too full of yourself; that's the reason you forgot about Grace, and that's the reason you want to be in the play. It's the bad blood in you, from your father." I burned inside. "You can tell that teacher of yours that you will not be in the play, and that's that."

Miss Campbell called the class to order. "I hope that those of you who went home for lunch remembered to give your mothers the instructions for the costumes for the Christmas play. As I call out your name, if your mother has agreed to make your costume, just answer, 'Yes, Miss Campbell.' "

I panicked. How could I explain that fifteen cents was too much for our household? And with the name "Brary" so close to the beginning of the alphabet, I was sure to be called on in a few moments. What would I say? If I…

"Sheila? Sheila Brary?"

"Yes, Miss Campbell?"

"Fine," she said happily and went on to the next name.

I slumped down in my seat. Oh, God. How had that happened?

When all the names had been called, Miss Campbell reached into the right-hand drawer of her desk and pulled out *Wind in the Willows*. She read aloud to us each day if we had behaved. All she had to do, if anyone was unruly, was to warn, "Keep that up, and I'll have to cancel our reading after lunch." Then the whole class would calm down.

She had us put our heads down on our folded arms. Her voice was pleasant and relaxed. In the background, the steam radiators clanked companionably.

"Nice? It's the only thing," said the Water Rat solemnly, as he leant forward for his stroke. "Believe me, my young friend, there is nothing—absolutely nothing—half so worth doing as simply messing about in boats. Simply messing," he went on dreamily: "messing—about—in—boats; messing…"

I agonized about how I'd let Miss Campbell think Mom was going to make my costume. Mom wouldn't change her mind I knew. I'd have to find some other way. Maybe I could earn the money to buy the cheesecloth by collecting old bottles. It would have to be a lot of bottles.

I thought about our neighbour who lived across the field behind our house, Mrs. Wadleigh. She liked to sew and had made a dress for me from an old discarded skirt of hers. And that was in spite of me throwing up on her clean kitchen floor one summer when I'd eaten too many radishes from our back yard.

"It's for Sheila to start grade two," she'd said when she'd brought it over. "I've made an extra-wide hem to let down. It should last her the school year."

The dress was so soft it crushed in my hand, and it was wine-coloured with a white Peter Pan collar embroidered with pink and crimson flowers. There was a second collar to tack on when the first was being laundered. This one had pointed tips and had yellow and green cross-stitching.

If I got the money and bought the cheesecloth, could I ask Mrs. Wadleigh to make the costume for me?

Heavy knocking at the front door pulled me up out of a deep sleep. I glanced at the front window, and it was still black night. The knocking came again, only louder. I was too scared to get up and answer the door, so I called out, "Mom! Mom!"

"What is it, Sheila?" Mom answered in a few moments, sleep dragging out her voice. The knocking continued, louder still. Mom got up to answer.

I heard the door open on its chain. "Who is it?" Mom called out.

"It's your next-door-neighbour, Mr. Bruce."

Mom took the chain off and let him in. "Whatever is it, Mr. Bruce, that brings you out this time of night?"

"It's about Mr. Powers. The hospital phoned." His voice dropped, and all I could hear was "hemorrhage" and "suddenly."

My mother's voice became hushed and sad. "Oh, I hate to waken the poor woman with news like this! She was out to see him not twenty-four hours ago. Would it be better, perhaps, if you were to tell her? You have the details."

Was Mr. Powers dead? I'd never seen him, and I had no face to put death on. I huddled down under the covers, feeling small and vulnerable. If Mr. Powers could die, then Mom could, too. Who would take care of us? Dad wouldn't stay around long enough to. Mom said so, and I felt that in my heart. There was no one else. I was filled with terror at the enormity of death and couldn't get my mind around it. What would we do? None of my mother's relatives lived close enough. As for Dad's, they lived in Saskatchewan, and Mom said that they had disowned him long ago as the black sheep of the family. We seldom heard from them. Mom had written last year, when Dad had pneumonia, to ask for help. When she received their reply, she let it drop from her fingers as if the paper burned her fingers. " 'So sorry,' they say, 'be sure to write us and let us know how Frank is doing.' What help is that? And giving me yet one more thing to do, as if I'm not at my wit's end now." I was so afraid of death that I used to wake up in the middle of the night and call out, "Mom, Mom, are you all right?" I needed to hear her voice to be sure she was still alive.

Mrs. Powers must have had some inkling of what had happened because when Mom tapped at her door, she came out of her room with a look of anguish on her face. Mom had to half-support her as they walked together into the kitchen.

I heard the chain of the kitchen light as it was pulled on, Mr. Bruce's deep rumble, the tap running, the kettle being filled. Mrs. Powers began to cry in a jagged way. It hurt to hear her.

The sky outside the front window was still dark when the rattle of the first streetcar of the day came around the loop. I got out of bed and began to dress quickly as Mrs. Powers' voice came floating into the living room. "I knew something wasn't quite right when I saw him yesterday morning. I knew it in my bones. Of course, they told me from the beginning that the disease would progress."

As I made my way into the kitchen, Mom was saying, "Mrs. Powers, if you want to leave Grace in our care while you make arrangements...."

"No, I'll take her back with me to my people in Olds. There's no point in staying in the city any longer. I'll pack our few things. I know I still owe you a week's rent, but I will send it to you just as soon as I get on my feet."

"Don't worry about it," Mom was quick to say. Yet I knew she had been counting on that money. She touched Mrs. Powers gently on the forearm. "In times like these, we all have to help wherever we can." I knew Mom was moved because normally she never touched people. She said it wasn't right to be that personal.

Mr. Bruce spoke. "When you're ready, Mrs. Powers, I'll give you a lift to the hospital." He stopped and made noises of clearing his throat. "To pick up your husband's belongings. And then on to the train station if you want."

"I'm obliged to you," said Mrs. Powers.

Mom caught sight of me. "Sheila, pour some more hot water on the tea. Then get Grace up and help her pack her things."

Grace was almost impossible to waken. Even when I had her standing on her feet, her eyes remained closed, and she swayed back and forth. But, finally, I got her dressed and her few belongings packed away into a brown paper bag.

As Grace, Mrs. Powers and Mr. Bruce were leaving, with Mom saying, "You will keep in touch?" I ran into the living room and reached up to the ledge for the empty chocolate box that held my favourite cutouts of the Dionne quintuplets. I tucked the box under Grace's arm. She looked at me blankly. "They're for you, Grace," I said. I wished I had been nicer to her before.

CHAPTER
three

D ad came home one midnight with two frozen jack-
rabbits he'd hit with his Ford during a snowstorm
on the highway between Edmonton and Calgary.
I heard the hard *thunk* as he let them drop onto the kitchen
table. The light from the kitchen made long shadows into the
living room where I lay half-awake on the chesterfield. A smell
of cigarette smoke and frying sausages drifted into the living
room, and I could hear the jouncing of the kettle's lid for tea.

A feeling of relief and happiness washed over me. The past
several weeks had seemed so long. Each day I'd expected the law
to catch up to me and charge me with the fire in the horse stables. Added to that was the new misery that I hadn't been able to
earn one penny, and I needed fifteen cents for the cheesecloth.

"And how are the kiddies?" I heard Dad ask Mom.

There was a rattle of cutlery. "They're fine. Except for
Sheila. That child will be the death of me. She's always into
something. She's taken to going to the United Church. It's
made me the laughing stock of the whole neighbourhood."

"Oh, come on now, Agnes. It doesn't mean a thing.
I wouldn't worry for two minutes about it."

"That's all very well for you to say. You're not here to have to deal with the children. No, you're off gallivanting, God knows where and with what woman. It's me that's left to worry about how to put a decent bite into their stomachs."

"For pity's sake, Agnes! Don't be that way. I've hardly got in the door, and already you've started in on me. I've been driving all day and all night. I'm tired out."

"I've no doubt that you're tired out, but it's not from driving. Why couldn't you have at least written? Is that asking too much?"

"I kept hoping I'd have some good news," Dad said. "I went out each day looking for a job, talking to this man and that, but none of the leads paid off. I barely made enough money to keep myself going."

"And what about us?" Mom's voice was shrill. "How were we supposed to manage?"

"I knew that you would, somehow. You always do. It's a great comfort to me to know the kiddies will be all right with you. I've never known anyone who has your knack, Agnes. You can make a home out of nothing."

"But to have at least had a note from you, Frank! Surely that was not asking too much. You couldn't afford one postage stamp?"

I put the pillow over my head. Dad was home again. It was enough.

~

After breakfast, Dad had presents for us all. Mine was a pink ribbon for my hair, and I ran to the bathroom to try it on in front of the mirror. "How do I look, Dad?" I asked when I returned, hoping he'd say I was pretty.

My mother spoke up. "It's not a good colour on you. Pink doesn't suit people with brown eyes."

Dad winced. "I think it suits you very well, Sheila," he said, "although maybe you should let your hair grow a little longer." Dad smiled at me, lines like chicken's feet at the corners of his eyes.

Mom snapped back. "I take all the children into the barber at the same time. I have him cut Sheila's hair short just like the boys.

"You should be glad we have a little girl," said Dad quietly.

My mother was not appeased. "Next thing you'll want is for her to have a finger wave, like some of your fancy girlfriends."

"There's just no sense talking to you, Agnes," Dad said as he pushed his chair back from the table, "not when you're in this mood. I'm going out."

"Where are you off to now?" Mom said, anxiety sharpening her eyes. "You're no sooner in this house than you want to be off again."

"I'm going out for some fresh air," Dad answered, "and I hope that by the time I get back you will have got yourself in hand. Because if you haven't, I'm going out again. Get your coat on, Sheila. You're coming with me. I want to hear about what you've been up to."

I felt caught between the two of them. In the end, I went with Dad. I glanced back at Mom as I left, hoping she wouldn't be too angry. I was shocked at her expression. She was looking at Dad with what seemed a small, triumphant smile.

"I just can't understand your mother," Dad said as we walked down the street. I gave a couple of hops, trying to match my steps to his. "She gets this bee in her bonnet, and then there's just no talking to her…I blame the Catholic Church. I think she would be all right if she didn't go along with all they say, but she swallows the whole kit and caboodle." He shook his head. "Such a waste! She has so much to offer, but, oh my, there's no pleasing her once she gets on the war path."

It didn't make me feel any better to have Dad talking about Mom that way than it did when she bad-mouthed him. I scuffed along, hoping he would change the subject.

"Pick up your feet, Sheila," he said. "If there's one thing I can't stand, it's someone who shuffles." I picked them up.

We met Mr. Green outside his house shovelling snow. "Good day to you, Mr. Green," said my father, touching his hat brim with his finger. "Looks like winter is settling in at last."

"I dunno about that," Mr. Green grunted, stopping long enough to send a stream of tobacco juice towards a snowbank where it left a punched-out hole of yellow. "I do know it's about time you got back, your kids running wild and all."

I felt my father stiffen beside me, but his voice was mild. "I'm not sure I catch the drift of what you're saying, Mr. Green."

"That big fire we had. Course, you were away, as per usual. Horses burned. Kids were roasting spuds in that empty lot next the horse stables, weren't they? It had to be a spark from their bonfire set the hay on fire."

My father's eyes hardened to the colour of the steel water tower behind the school. "I see," he said slowly. "Well, kids will be kids. Where were the adults all this time? Did any of them check that the fire was out? Why do you blame the kiddies?"

Mr. Green sent another jet of tobacco juice into the snowbank. Now there were two holes, like the eyes of a tiger. "That's not the point," he said testily. "Fires is dangerous things. Kids shouldn't be allowed to have them. That's my contention."

"Mighty interesting, Bill Green," Dad said. "Particularly since I remember that last fall, you decided to burn off a little prairie wool on the field behind. Do you remember that? You wanted to plant a few potatoes, you said, come spring. It ended up with the whole damn neighbourhood having to go out with gunny sacks, and we spent the afternoon putting out the fire."

I stared up at Dad. He never swore. My eyes switched to Mr. Green whose face had blotches of purple. He began to splutter, as if strangling on his tobacco juice.

"Good day to you, sir," Dad said. This time he didn't bother to touch his finger to his hat.

When we were out of hearing, I tugged at Dad's coat sleeve. "Dad, did you know I gave the boys the matches for the bonfire?" I said, the words tumbling out. "They didn't have any, and they asked me to get some. It was that fire…the horses…Mom said—" I couldn't say the words. "We're not supposed to touch the matches," I finished in a small voice.

"That's because they cost money, and they are not play things," Dad answered, but he didn't sound shocked.

"Didn't Mom tell you? How it was all my fault?"

"Your fault, what?" He stopped walking to turn and stare at me.

"That the fire started in the stables," I wailed. "And now the horses are dead. I did it."

"For the love of Mike!" he said with a look of stunned disbelief on his face. "How could you ever think such a thing?"

"Mom said if I hadn't taken the matches in the first place and given them to the boys—"

"Oh, no, honey, you can't take on the guilt of the whole world. The boys shouldn't have asked you for the matches in the first place. It was their idea to have a fire, and it was up to them to make sure it was out. Everyone knows that. Now, don't you give it a second thought. Though, in the future, I wouldn't get matches for anyone. Let them get their own matches." He shook his head. Then, under his breath, "God Almighty, to make a kiddie feel guilty about *that*."

Twice in one day he'd sworn. "Oh, what a relief!" I shouted out loud and took a running slide down the icy sidewalk, twirling and letting myself drop in a snowbank with outstretched arms. I had been absolved, and I was free to make a snow angel under the pure blue sky.

Dad came alongside me. "Let's go downtown," he said. "We can look at the Christmas decorations in the stores and have something to eat at Hudson's Bay."

Our street was on the streetcar loop, and we didn't have long to wait before a streetcar rumbled to the corner. We sat beside steamy windows, transfers in our hands, and swayed on the hard leather seats at every corner. The streetcar clattered across Louise bridge, the Bow River motionless below, locked in ice. On Eighth Avenue, the stores were bright with Christmas decorations and coloured lights.

Over hot chocolate at Hudson's Bay's lunch counter in the basement, I told Dad about the upcoming Christmas play. "I'm supposed to be Mary," I explained, "and I need a costume. I asked Mom, but she said we can't afford it. I've been trying and trying to find a way to earn the fifteen cents I need to buy the cheesecloth. I thought maybe Mrs. Wadleigh would show me how to sew the costume."

"Well, Sheila, if that's all you need—"

Just then a woman stopped beside us and cried out with obvious delight, "Why, Frank Brary, I didn't know you were back in the city!" She was about the same age as Mom, but there the resemblance ended. She wore two spots of reddish-orange rouge. Her hair looked dull, the colour flat, as if she dyed it. There was a smell of sweet-pea perfume, stale and cheap. I sensed an undercurrent between Dad and her. "And who's the little girl? Don't tell me she's yours. Why, Frank, you old devil." She laughed as she slipped onto the empty stool next to him.

Then, in what seemed no time at all, Dad turned to me and said, "Finish up your hot chocolate. Irene and I have a lot of news to catch up on, and we're going over to her place for a little visit."

"It's not far from here, Frank," Irene said as we left, "and I can offer you something a little stronger than hot chocolate."

CHAPTER
four

I rene lived two blocks away from Hudson's Bay in a tall, narrow house—like an upended shoebox—near the river. The house seemed to lean to one side, and a couple of the front steps sagged under our feet. The window to the right of the door was patched with cardboard. Inside the house was a strong, musty odour, as if the river had overflowed its banks one spring and flooded the basement. I followed Dad and Irene up to the top floor. Around me were the sounds of the house: radios, glasses clinking and uneven bursts of conversation behind closed doors. The last flight of stairs—so narrow and steep that it reminded me of a ladder—led directly into Irene's room.

The room was filled with stuffed pillows. They lay on the Winnipeg couch, the chairs, the floor, everywhere. They bore the names of Banff, Jasper, Lake Louise, Montana, the Calgary Stampede and the Kicking Horse Pass. Irene kept asking me questions, but I barely answered because I was so busy looking around me. There were celluloid dolls with crocheted dresses perched in the spots not occupied by pillows. Photographs were tucked into the frame of the dresser mirror: Irene leaning on the hood of a late model Ford, Irene and girlfriend with arms around each other, Irene dressed in a low-cut gown and holding a harlequin mask up to her eyes. Face powder spilled across the top of the dresser. Hair snarled in a brush. In the corners of the room, dust balls rolled.

"Sheila, you're a million miles away," Dad's voice called me back. "Irene asked you a question, honey."

"She's probably noticing what a rotten housekeeper I am. Oh, well, there are more important things in life than keeping a place all spiffied up, I say." She lit a cigarette, something I'd never seen a woman do before, except in the movies. "So, Sheila, what part do you have in this school play your dad's been telling me about?"

"Mary, the mother of Jesus."

She choked on her cigarette smoke. Then, "Your dad says you need a costume, and you're having trouble getting one."

I bent my head, embarrassed. Why had he told her?

"I've got all sorts of odds and ends around here. You can see that for yourself." She let out a whoop of laughter. "Got a sewing machine. I could run you up a costume in no time flat. That's if you'd like me to." She sounded wistful, as if she wanted me to like her.

"What do you say, Sheila?" said Dad. "Isn't that pretty nice of Irene?"

"Yes. Thank you." My stomach had tightened into a hard ball.

"I could have it done in about a week," said Irene, flicking ash onto the linoleum floor. "Here, stand up on this chair, and I'll take a few measurements."

"Oh, I don't think so—"

"Come on, honey," Dad said, squeezing my upper arm. "You don't want to keep Irene waiting."

My father watched with a pleased look as Irene took a tape and measured me from shoulder to knee, shoulder to waist, and then around my chest. I broke out in a sweat having her touch me.

While Irene wrote down the measurements, Dad handed me a nickel. "Why don't you wander back to Hudson's Bay for an hour or so, Sheila. Buy yourself something you like. I'll lend you my watch, so you can keep track of the time. You don't need to be back for an hour. Don't hurry, take your time. Irene and I have things we want to talk about, and we don't want to be interrupted. Okay, sweetheart?"

He dipped into the watch pocket of his vest and pulled out his watch dangling on its silver chain. The watch felt warm from his body.

I clumped down the stairs, out onto the street, and back to Hudson's Bay, this time deliberately shuffling my feet. I didn't care if my father couldn't stand it. I couldn't stand what was happening.

I was gripping the nickel so hard that it cut into my hand. I opened my hand and looked at the coin. Five cents. Still ten cents short from buying the material for the costume.

A Salvation Army woman, dressed in a blue bonnet and long blue dress, stood outside the glass doors of Hudson's Bay and rang her bell at the passing crowd. People averted their eyes from the large open kettle at her feet that held only a few pennies. I wondered what Dad and Irene were doing.

The nickel felt dirty in my hand. I threw it in the kettle where it spun around a couple of times before settling.

"God bless you, child," the Salvation Army woman sang out, and she rang her bell with renewed vigour.

I pushed my way into Hudson's Bay and then up the escalator to the toy floor. Rows and rows of Shirley Temple dolls smiled vacantly at me from the shelves behind the counter. I leaned forward to check the price tags. Even the smallest cost nine dollars. One, in a pink organdy dress with matching hair bow, and wearing white shoes, cost sixteen.

Near the dolls was a stage, and Santa sat there with a small boy on his knee, the mother hovering on the sidelines. When the boy rejoined his mother, Santa noticed me and beckoned. I didn't believe in Santa anymore. Billy Bruce had set me straight on that when I was five. But I had nothing else to do, so I climbed the three little stairs.

"And have *you* been a good girl this year?" he asked. His brown eyes were bloodshot.

I thought of all the times I'd been in trouble with Mom. And the time I beat up Tom. "Not very," I said.

"*Ho, Ho, Ho.* I'm sure you have. And what would you like for Christmas?" Then, in an undertone as he fingered his eyebrows, his beard, "What are you looking at?"

"Were you at Eaton's last year?"

"Santa is everywhere. *Ho, Ho, Ho.* It's part of his magic."

"But you had blue eyes at Eaton's."

He grunted and nudged me along. Then he turned to greet another child. "Who's this cute little tyke coming to see her old friend, Santa?" he called out. A girl about five came shining towards him, her mother smiling, tears making her eyes like stars.

I wandered over to the area of the toy department where the books were displayed. *Nancy Drew, Anne of Green Gables.* Then I saw a picture book, *The Nativity Story,* and I reached for it. As I was turning the pages, studying the way Mary was dressed, a saleswoman came over. "Are you interested in buying the book?" she asked.

"How much is it?" I stalled.

"Twenty-five cents."

"Well, I've just given away all my money to the Salvation Army. I'll have to come in another day," I said. Her thin eyebrows peaked as if she didn't believe me.

Once again, I found myself standing outside on the busy street. The Salvation Army woman had been joined by three men, also in uniform. They had brought a bugle, trumpet and drum and had set up music stands in a semi-circle behind the woman. After a few minutes of practice, they launched into a blustery "Onward Christian Soldiers." It was so loud it sent me back into the store.

The hat department looked interesting. I tried on several hats. "If you're not planning to buy a hat, would you please not handle the merchandise?" the saleswoman said, but her look was sympathetic. "I know," she said in a low voice, "we females seem to have a special need to try on hats. But please don't get me into trouble. Jobs are too hard to come by."

I took my father's watch from my pocket. The hour was up. "I don't have any more time, anyway," I said.

I stomped up the last flight of stairs to Irene's room, making as much noise as possible. Inside, my father was lying on the couch smoking a cigarette. Smoke rings of increasing sizes floated above his head. I heard the distant flush and gurgle of water in pipes, and Irene came up the stairs a few minutes later, carrying a towel over her arm. Both Irene and Dad looked soft and relaxed and pleased with themselves, as if they shared a secret. My stomach began to hurt again.

"Help yourself to some cookies, Sheila," Irene said. A plate of cookies, a glass of milk and a tin teapot waited on the table.

The cookies, store-bought, tasted stale and artificial. My mother made better ones, with raisins. Irene reached over and took the package of tailor-made cigarettes from Dad's shirt pocket, letting her hand linger there for a moment. I almost choked. How *could* Dad like this woman better than my mother? Mom was always clean. Irene's neck had a grimy ring around it. Even the way they dressed was different. Mom wore loose housedresses; Irene's skirt was too tight. Her sweater showed off her breasts separately, not in a comfortable mound like my mother's, and Irene's looked hard and jutting, as if they could stab you in the eye if you got too close.

"Did you buy anything at the store, honey?" Dad's voice was as lazy as his cigarette smoke that drifted upwards in the stale air.

"No." There was an odd smell in the room, like bleach.

"Still have your money, then? Going to save it? That's a good girl."

"I gave it to the Salvation Army. I put it in their Christmas kettle."

"Whoops!" Irene sputtered, "there's a little insurance for you, Frank." My dad laughed, having a good time, dragging it out for all it was worth. I couldn't wait to get out of that room and go home. I hated being part of what they were doing.

It seemed forever before my father stood, stretched. "We must be on our way, Irene. Not that I haven't enjoyed the visit."

Irene saw us to the door. The odd smell was coming from her, too. *Fusty.* "See you in a week, then? Sheila's costume should be ready by then."

I groaned inside. Without even trying, I'd become involved in what they were doing. This was not the way I had hoped Dad would help me.

"Don't forget your manners, Sheila," Dad reminded me.

"Thank you for the cookies," I said, not looking at Irene but down at the floor. "They were very nice."

"And for your help with the costume," Dad prompted.

"Yes, that, too." Then, looking up at Irene and saying it quickly so I wouldn't lose courage, "You don't have to go to the trouble. I'll find another way. Thank you very much, just the same."

"Don't worry about your mother," Irene's tone was matter-of-fact. "It will be our little secret, between the three of us."

I rushed away from them both and down the stairs, anxious to be out in the clean air. I couldn't seem to get enough breath, my chest tight with wanting to cry.

Dad caught up to me at the streetcar shelter at the end of the street. "There's no need for you to say anything about this afternoon to your mother. She wouldn't understand. Just wear the costume Irene makes for you. If your mother asks, tell her I got it for you, but you don't know where."

I couldn't answer him. My throat ached from holding back tears.

It was dusk by the time we got off the streetcar near home, and the late afternoon sun had bruised the sky red and purple. We walked in silence to our house.

As soon as my mother saw us come in the back door, she drained the potatoes at the sink. I could hear my brothers in the bathroom, washing up. Mom hadn't spoken yet, but the unasked questions showed in her stiffened shoulders. When we all sat down to eat, the pressure in the air was like that just before a thunderstorm.

"This is a nice bit of rabbit stew, Agnes," my father said, his fork to his mouth. "Not many women have your talent for making a home. On next to nothing, too. This Depression…. Laws amassey. Will it never end? The farmers around Edmonton were telling me that it costs more to ship their cream into the city than what they're eventually paid for it. I don't know what those people in Ottawa are doing to help the working-man. The relief camps aren't worth a pinch of gopher—"

"Frank," Mom warned, "the children." But her face had softened a little. "There's a Social Credit meeting tomorrow afternoon," she said, "and William Aberhart's going to be there."

"I have no more faith in Aberhart than in any of the other politicians," Dad said. "I know you do, Agnes, because he's a preacher. But as far as I'm concerned, they're all a bunch of crooks." He caught sight of the displeasure on Mom's face.

"I do admire you for keeping up with politics the way you do, even with all the work with the house and kiddies. Why don't you go to the meeting? I'll take care of things here. The kids like my cooking. You can come home to a meal cooked by someone else for a change."

"That would be nice," Mom said, with a half-smile hovering around her mouth. I hadn't seen Mom smile for a long time. "I've not been out of the house for a month. There's custard pie for dessert. I know you like it, and at least eggs and milk are cheap."

My mother got up from the table to fetch the pie, her face animated and her movements brisk. We all brightened up with the change in her mood.

~

It wasn't until I was washing my face at bedtime, and my mother appeared at the bathroom door, that the cloud of the afternoon rolled back.

"I was just wondering, Sheila," she said in a casual tone, "where you and your father were all afternoon?" She leaned against the doorjamb, as if this were just a friendly conversation.

"Like Dad said. We went downtown to look at the Christmas decorations."

"For six hours?" Mom moved into the bathroom and peered into my face.

"At Hudson's Bay, I saw Santa Claus and looked through the toy department at the books and everything.

"All that time and *nothing* to eat? I noticed you didn't eat much supper."

"I don't much like rabbit, not after I watched Dad skin it, all that white fur."

"No mashed potatoes? No dessert?"

There was no escape from those piercing eyes. "We stopped and had hot chocolate at Hudson's Bay."

"You must have had something more than that."

"No," I said, thinking unhappily of Irene's store-bought cookies. "I guess I wasn't very hungry at supper."

"You who always clean off your plate and then look around for more? You're lying to me, Sheila. I can always tell. Your father must have met someone he knew. All of you went somewhere to eat. Isn't that closer to the truth? That's it, isn't it?" she demanded in a louder voice. "And—knowing him—it was bound to be a woman."

"Oh, Mom…"

"If you had any decency, or appreciation of how hard I work to keep this home together, you would know where your loyalties lie."

I ducked my head and washed my face again, then groped for the towel. Keeping my face buried in it, my voice came out muffled. "Ask Dad, not me."

"So he can lie, too? You ought to be ashamed of yourself, trying to protect him. A lot he cares for you! Oh, I know, you think he's so wonderful and that I'm so bad. If he really cared for you, he'd be at home where he belongs, not roaming around the countryside, spending on everyone else but us."

Even after I went to bed and pulled the covers up over my head, Mom kept on at me. Then Dad came into the living room, and she fell silent.

Paul wandered in soon after that. He lifted the covers from my head and whispered, "Billy Bruce told me today that he was the one who asked you to get the matches and that you hadn't wanted to." I lay very still. "I heard Mom blaming you," Paul went on. "But it was Billy's fault, not yours, and we should have made sure the fire was out. Next time anybody asks you to do something you don't want to, you just tell them your brother Paul says you don't have to, and then you tell me."

five

Mom opened Saturday's *Calgary Herald*—the Bruces passed it on to us when they were through with it—and spread it out on the kitchen table. She turned to the classified section.

"Listen to this," she said to Dad. " 'Looking for good mechanic. Steam and gas tickets.' It's a downtown address…. I wonder if anyone would be there on a Sunday?"

Dad took the paper to see for himself. "I guess I could give it a try. But here's an interesting one. 'Lethbridge. Dairyman wanted, Holsteins, twenty-five head.' "

"That's out of the city!" Mom protested, sounding hurt.

There was a knock at the back door. Martha Beryl wanted me to go to Sunday School with her.

"Sunday School?" Mom said, not bothering to hide her displeasure. "You mean our Sheila at the United Church?"

"What does it matter, Agnes?" Dad said mildly. "Let her go. Surely it's the same God almighty who looks after all of us."

"A fine one you are to talk! You haven't set foot in a church in years."

"You run along, honey," Dad said, giving me a pat on the shoulder. Then, turning back to my mother, "Sometimes, Agnes, I think that Saint Peter himself would be hard-pressed to get along with you. You must lie awake at night figuring out how miserable you can be the next day."

"Let's go," I said quickly to Martha, not wanting her to hear anymore.

Mom's strident voice followed us out the door. "I suppose you'd rather take the dairyman job, Frank. Out of sight, out of mind."

"I'm going downtown, Agnes. Anything to get away from your harping." I glanced sideways at Martha. She looked embarrassed, and I shrivelled inside.

~

It was after midnight before Dad came in the front door. He stumbled, swore, bumped into furniture, and then swore again. As he passed by the chesterfield where I lay, I smelled a strange odour, like overripe fruit.

I heard him go into the bathroom and crash around. After a while he came out and made his way unsteadily to the front bedroom.

By that time, I had to go to the bathroom myself. When I switched on the light, I saw that my father had been sick all over the floor.

Mom joined me in the doorway as I stood there wondering how I was going to reach the toilet without getting my feet in the mess. She didn't say anything, but she looked disgusted. Fetching a pail, old rags and newspapers, she cleaned up the vomit. I shivered. I vowed I would never be the wife of a drunken husband.

"He didn't get the job," Mom muttered through clenched teeth. "So, of course, he had to have a few drinks with his so-called friends."

She put her hands to the small of her back and arched back, as if to relieve pain. "The city is threatening to cut off the gas and electricity because of late payments. I'll have to go down to the City Hall first thing in the morning and apply for relief. We can't go on like this."

~

"I don't understand it, Sheila," said Miss Campbell. "You live less than a block away, and yet you are late after lunch."

How could I possibly explain Mom and Dad's latest row?

Martha, who sat behind me, slipped me a note. "Where were you? I called and called."

"Now, class," Miss Campbell was saying, "before we open our *Highroads to Reading*, I'd like to talk to you briefly about the Christmas play, and also about the meaning of Christmas. It's about giving. God gave his Son to the world. The wise men gave gifts to this Son. We all have gifts that we can give and not just at Christmas, either. They needn't be expensive gifts, but the gifts should come from our hearts." She paused and looked around the classroom, her eyes settling on me. "Sheila, you're going to be Mary. What gift does Mary give to her baby?"

"A mother's love?"

"Yes, certainly that, a mother's love. And you, Martha. As an angel, what gift could an angel give to the Christ child?"

I heard Martha's wheeze as she tried to take a deep breath, then silence.

I leaned back in my seat and shielded my mouth with my hand. "You could be His guardian angel," I whispered.

"I could be His guardian angel," Martha said loudly.

"Sheila," scolded Miss Campbell, "you know the rule about whispering. Go sit on the stool in the corner."

There were a few titters as I walked to the corner behind the teacher's desk and sat on the high wooden stool, facing the wall. Twice in one morning I'd displeased Miss Campbell. Tears plopped down on my dress, were absorbed into the wool.

Behind me, Miss Campbell's voice had become brisk and cheerful again. "Now, how are the costumes coming along? How about yours, Martha?"

"It's almost finished, Miss Campbell."

"Very good." Miss Campbell went down each row checking: the shepherds, the sheep, everyone was asked in turn. Except me. Miss Campbell seemed to have forgotten that I was sitting in the corner behind her. I began to wonder if maybe I had a guardian angel after all, the way Mom said. But then, Mom believed in leprechauns and fairies, too. She told us stories of fairy rings on her great-aunts' farm in Pomeroy, County Tyronne, and of a little old woman who came to their cottage one morning and asked for a cup of buttermilk. "After she drank the buttermilk, she took Great Aunt Eliza's hand. Eliza said there were no bones in the hand. It was like cotton wool. Eliza fainted to the ground when she realized the old woman was a fairy in disguise." I didn't believe the story but felt uneasy just in case. I tried hard to dismiss my mother's stories as not being Canadian. It was bad enough that I mispronounced many words at school, words like "oven" and "calm," giving them her Irish accent so that they came out "ah-ven" and "cam." One of her stories that I hated was that my Grandmother McConnell, who had died last year, could see everything I did. I went around for months haunted by the thought that she could even see me picking my nose. I could never shake the feeling of being, in some small perpetual way, wicked.

Sitting there with my feet hooked on the rungs of the stool, I decided that, instead of counting on a guardian angel— which may or may not be true—I would go over the field to see Mrs. Wadleigh and ask for her help with my costume.

But then she would be sure to tell my mother. All the women in the neighbourhood did that, stuck together when it came to children and husbands who harboured secrets.

When I got home after school, Mom was at the stove lifting the lid off a small pan. The smell of simmering finnan haddie sweetened the air, smelling like birch wood smoke. Two bags of groceries sat on the counter beside the sink.

"Put the groceries away for me, Sheila, there's a good girl."

"You got the relief money, then?" I asked, thinking that maybe now Mom could spare the fifteen cents for my costume.

"Yes, but I don't want it talked about all over the neighbourhood. Now, I mean that! We all know how you can't keep a thing to yourself."

Was that true?

"I remember when you started school," she said. "You told the school nurse that you only had one bath a month. I had a hard time convincing her that, indeed, you had one every week."

"It did seem like a month to me."

"Well, you are to be quiet about us being on relief."

Then her face crumpled as she cried out, "Having to stand in line for almost two hours, and then questions at the end of it, like I was some sort of criminal. But at least I got some help, enough to tide us over for a little while."

Her voice rose with indignation. "Mr. Pritchard, though, will have to wait another month for his mortgage payments. Well, he can afford to. He's got more money than he knows what to do with, and there's no one dependent on him."

I'd met Mr. Pritchard a few times, a tiny, wizened old man who gave me lint-covered peppermints from his jacket pocket.

"No," Mom said. "It wouldn't hurt him the slightest to give us a little leeway." She reached into the warming oven for the plates. "Call the boys for supper, Sheila. Your father's not home yet, but I won't wait for him again."

Dad didn't come home for supper. No one mentioned his absence, but his empty chair seemed like a touch of blight in our kitchen.

I went to sleep that night tight with misery, thinking that Irene could be making the costume for me that very minute, and there was nothing I could do to stop her. Dad was probably there now, sitting among the stuffed cushions.

About ten that evening, Tom woke up with a toothache. Mom put oil of cloves on a piece of cotton wool and packed it into the cavity. "That tooth will have to be seen to," she said. "I'll send a note to Nurse Gunn at the school tomorrow and see if she can get a voucher for the dentist."

I couldn't get back to sleep with Dad not home yet. Bad things had a way of happening at our house during the night, and I was always afraid to let go and fall asleep.

I am three and sleep on a cot at the foot of my parents' bed. I'm half-wakened by the sound of my mother's voice protesting.

"Oh, no!" my mother cries. "You can't come in at this time of the night and expect me to—"

"Now Agnes, don't be like that," Dad coaxes. "Hush.... Come on, now."

But whatever it is, my mother isn't having any. The more my father insists, the louder Mom's voice until finally she is shrieking, "Children! Help! CHILDREN! HELP ME!"

The overhead light goes on. The naked bulb swings back and forth on its cord. Its glare, like an eye, shows my mother lying in bed, my father half-crouched over her. She is crying and pushing him away. When she sees me standing upright on my cot, she begins screaming again.

I start to scream, too, as loud as I can. Dad drops back on his heels, but not looking around, says, "Stop it, Sheila. This has nothing to do with you."

Paul is huddled at the bedroom door, a slingshot in his hand. "Leave Mom alone!" he tells Dad, but his voice breaks near the end of the sentence, as if he is crying inside.

My father sits down on the edge of the bed and rests one elbow on his knee, his forehead in the palm of his hand. "Go back to sleep, both of you," he says wearily.

"Your mother is having hysterics again."

At this, Mom gets out of bed, pushes past him, and makes her way to the front door. I pad behind her, the linoleum floor cold under my feet. She takes down her coat from the hook and thrusts her bare feet into a pair of overshoes.

"Hysterics, is it?" she shouts back at Dad. "You coming in at three o'clock in the morning from one of your fancy ladies and thinking you can be with me, too?"

She goes out into the night, leaving Paul and me staring at each other. I go over to stand close to him. It seems a long time before she returns, and when she does, she has a policeman with her. Paul puts the slingshot behind his back.

My father, who has stayed seated on the edge of the bed, stands up and runs his fingers through his hair. "There really is no problem here," he says.

"No problem?" says the policeman, disbelief in his voice. "Your wife...expecting a baby...the neighbours disturbed...a phone call for help...."

He spots me. "Your little girl crying her heart out because her parents can't get along. Oh, yes, sir, I think there is some problem here." He seems to fill the room with his dark uniform and heavy voice. I am so glad of his presence that I begin to hiccup with relief.

Paul goes back to the bedroom he shares with Tom and Andy. Mom comes over to stand beside me and pushes the hair back from my forehead. "Just see how badly he's frightened this poor child."

The policeman makes a few entries in his notebook. Then he says, "I think you should all go back to bed and go to sleep. It will all look different to you in the morning. And you, sir, don't bother your wife in any way tonight. She's tired out and needs her rest. Will you promise me that?"

"Oh, I can easily do that," says my father, but his voice sounds sarcastic. My mother looks at him, her face tightening with hate. I begin to cry again.

"There now, you two," the policeman says sternly to my parents. "Will you just settle down? If I were lucky enough to have such a nice family as you do—a little girl and all—I'd take care that nothing like this ever happened. You don't know how lucky you are."

I want him to stay, live with us, make my parents behave.

I am still crying when he leaves. My father goes with him to the front door. "There won't be any further problem, not on my part," Dad says. "You have my word on that."

As soon as the front door closes after the policeman, but before my father comes back to the bedroom, my mother comes over to me. She bends down and hisses, "You can stop your crying, now. I don't need you anymore."

I can't breathe. I will die from this.

Long after the house settles and my parents' breathing slows and they are asleep, I am wide awake, my eyes staring.

I am still awake when the first streetcar screeches around the loop. I pull on my clothes and go outside to the front porch.

There is a white band of sky along the southeastern horizon. I keep my eyes on it as it widens and turns the palest pink. Until now, I have always thought the world such a beautiful place, but now the weight of the sky presses down on me.

I am aware of the presence of evil. It is behind the clouds. It paints the tree trunks black and twists their branches until they look like menacing claws. Now I know that this evil has always been here. This is just the first time that I've seen it.

The day lurches forward as the milkman's wagon comes down the street. In the distance, the wagon is black, the horse a ghost.

The whole day drags on. Normal, everyday sounds explode around me. I search people's faces looking for something sinister lurking behind the eyes. Is that a twist to the mouth?

By nighttime, I ache all over. If anyone were to touch me, I would disintegrate.

The next morning dawns clear and bright. The trees have shrunk to their normal size, and their branches arch silver against a blue sky that is high and serene. The world has settled back on its axis.

CHAPTER SIX

The next Saturday, Dad said, "Get yourself prettied up, Sheila. I'm going downtown this afternoon, and you can come with me."

Mom looked up at him with sharp eyes. She let her mending drop in her lap. "I wanted Sheila to help around the house today."

"Let Tom do it," suggested Dad.

"Tom do a girl's work? That's Sheila's job.… You're forever spoiling that girl. You give her ideas about herself that turn her head. They'll bring her nothing but grief in the long run. It's no wonder I have so much trouble with her."

"Agnes, there's no reason on the face of this earth why you shouldn't give Sheila a chance once in a while. You're altogether too hard on her."

"Hard on her, is it? You're someone to talk about being hard. How hard are you on me? I work and slave in this house twenty-four hours a day, seven days a week, and how often do you take *me* downtown?"

"Come with us now," was Dad's reply.

"You know I can't. There's so much work to do, and no one else to do it."

"Ask Tom or Paul."

"I told you. It's women's work."

My father shrugged. "Have it your own way, then."

"Why are you going downtown?" Mom persisted. "There's precious little money for Christmas shopping, so you can't use that for an excuse."

"There's a man I want to see about a job. It's out of town, but it can't be helped. I've looked all over this city, and jobs are scarce as hens' teeth. If I'm going to get any kind of work, it won't be here in Calgary."

Mom picked up her mending. Her needle jabbed back and forth viciously.

"Okay, Snooks," Dad said to me, "get yourself ready. We leave in five minutes."

Dad shaved, patted some lotion on his face, then talcum powder. He leaned forward to take a closer look in the mirror and clipped a nose hair with the nail scissors. My stomach lurched. We were going to see Irene.

Irene must have been watching for us because she had the front door open before we were even up the steps. She was wearing a red see-through blouse, with a black bra under it, and Dad couldn't keep his eyes away. I heard him give a kind of grunt, and Irene laughed. By the time we reached the top of the stairs, Dad seemed to be breathing hard, which made Irene laugh again. They seemed to forget that I was there. I began chattering, trying to break the spell between them.

Once I was inside Irene's room, I had something worse to think about. There, draped over the back of a couch, was the costume Irene had made for me. It was bright orange.

"I couldn't get any brown cheesecloth," Irene said. "I would have settled for beige, but they didn't have any. But this should look pretty on you with your dark hair and eyes. Why don't you try it on and see how it fits?" She looked anxious, as if she wanted me to like the costume, and her, too. My father looked proud that she had gone to so much trouble for him.

Reluctantly, I slipped the costume over my head. "Why, Sheila," Dad said. "You do look pretty!"

Irene took me over to the full-length mirror that stood in the corner of the room. "See? Didn't I tell you?"

The robe was the right size, and the colour—instead of looking garish as it had on the back of the couch—was soft and glowing. I turned around, craning my neck, to view it from the back.

"Irene, you're a wonder," Dad said in a voice like butterscotch.

"Well, I *am* a professional dressmaker, after all."

"Say 'thank you' to Irene, honey," Dad reminded me.

They had settled themselves on the couch. Dad's arm lay along its back, his hand dangling so that his fingers touched Irene's shoulders.

"Thank you," I said, forcing the words out. "It was very kind of you."

"Why don't you go on out for a walk now, Sheila?" Dad said. "Irene and I have things to talk about. Take my watch and come back in an hour. Then Irene can parcel up the costume, and we'll take it with us." I wondered how we were going to get the parcel past my mother, but Dad seemed to know how to do these things.

I spent the next hour wandering around the downtown stores, pretending that I had lots of money and that I could buy whatever I wanted as presents for my family. I would buy my mother a big white house with cupboards full of food. I would replace the piano she'd had to sell with a grand piano. We would have the floors covered with Armstrong linoleum, like in the ads, a different pattern for each room. Dad would be happy to come home every night in time for supper. He would never do anything that would make Mom unhappy. I would never cause my mother any problems, and she would be happy with me in this perfect house.

I was still half-lost in this daydream when I went back to Irene's. I watched her wrap the costume, first in tissue paper, then brown.

Dusk was dropping quickly over the city as Dad and I left, a purple blind being pulled down over the window of sky. One by one, the street lamps flickered on. Even the sounds of the city seemed to drop half an octave with the ending of the day.

The streetcar was crowded. We passed old houses similar to Irene's, and I could look straight into the lighted rooms. One man sat alone at a table eating his dinner. His room was close enough to the streetcar tracks that I could see him raise a forkful of fried onions to his mouth. We ate fried onions at our house. If we ate the same things as other people, did that mean our thoughts were the same thoughts as other people's? Did this man sometimes worry, the way I was worrying now about Mom? And if so, that must mean that all people were the same, underneath.

Dad started to whistle as soon as we stepped down from the streetcar at our corner. I knew the song; it was on the radio all the time. "Oo-oo-oo, what a little moonlight can do for you-oo." My mother called such songs "nonsense" and didn't like to hear us sing them.

I followed Dad down the cinder path to our back door. He slipped the brown paper parcel inside his overcoat pocket before putting his hand on the knob. I skulked in behind him.

Mom, wearing her best dress, was moving briskly around the kitchen. "I'm going out to the movies," she said. "Paul and Tom are coming with me. There's a double feature on at the Crescent, Bette Davis and Clark Gable, and this is the week the Crescent's giving out free dinner plates."

"That's fine, Agnes," said Dad, smoothly. "You run along and enjoy yourself."

"There are wieners and scalloped potatoes in the warming oven." I was afraid Mom would look into my eyes and see the guilt I felt. But she was elated at going out, and she pulled on her woollen gloves without a second glance my way.

As soon as the door closed behind her, Dad handed me Irene's parcel. I hid it under the cushions of the chesterfield where I slept, to take to school Monday morning. I fell asleep that night, the presence of the orange robe burning through the cushions like a branding iron.

The next morning, Mom was so full of the movies she'd seen that she didn't seem to notice how quiet I was, or that I didn't eat much porridge. "That Bette Davis is a real Jezebel, but she got her just desserts at the end," Mom told us happily.

"It did you good to go out to the movies last night," Dad said. "You should go every week. I've always said that life is to be enjoyed whatever way we can. Times are tough, all right, but movies are cheaper than medicine. And you'll be glad to know that I'm going to give another shot at getting a job here in the city. I'll get up bright and early Monday morning and go downtown."

On Monday morning, I hid the costume under my coat and started off to school, glad to get it out of the house. It had been like a bomb ticking away under the chesterfield cushions.

Miss Campbell liked the robe, even though it was orange. She shook out the folds and held the dress at arm's length. "It's very nicely done. I had no idea your mother was such an accomplished seamstress. I must congratulate her." I rubbed my hands nervously down the skirt of my dress.

"My mother didn't actually make it," I said, my voice quavering. "It was a friend of...the family's."

"How nice to have such a friend. I'll put it away in this cupboard for now. Sheila, since you're here a little early this morning, would you pass out these papers for me? Put one on each desk."

~

Even though Dad looked for a job every day, there were none. And each day that passed made him more restless. "I'm going to take a run up to Red Deer," he told Mom. "I've heard there's a garage up there that needs a mechanic. Their mechanic had an accident. A car rolled back and crushed his foot."

"Where did you hear that?" Mom wanted to know.

"From Bill Green. It was his nephew that was hurt."

"It's an ill wind, they say. Do you want me to pack something for you to eat along the way? I have some pickled pigs' feet and half a raisin pie."

"That sounds mighty fine to me," Dad said. "I'll be sure to be back home for Christmas, and I'll bring presents for everyone. I've got a hunch I'm going to land this job."

"I hope not like the hunches you have every time you buy a ticket on the Irish Sweepstakes."

"My bad luck can't last forever. One of these days my ship will come in. You'll see."

Dad would be away for the school Christmas concert. If only it were Mom who couldn't go.

~

We had rehearsals after school all that week, but I never mentioned them at home. Instead, I told Mom I was at Martha's.

At our last rehearsal, we tried on our costumes. Delighted, Miss Campbell clapped her hands. "It all seems more real," she said. The manger was still empty, but it was easy to imagine a newborn baby there. It was easy, too, to imagine the applause we would get, how good it would sound.

When the day of the concert finally came, and Mom still hadn't said anything about going, I began to think that maybe I'd been granted a reprieve.

But after the supper dishes had been done and put away, Mom said, "I'm taking Tom to the concert tonight. He would enjoy it, I'm sure." I felt as though I'd fallen into the icy slough back of the hills, the one people said had quicksand.

The only thing I could hope for was that Mom would leave early, before our play started. *If not that, please dear God, don't let Mom have a chance to talk to Miss Campbell.* Maybe I could just get sick, miss the whole play. Or I could say that Miss Campbell had supplied the costume. I'd have to do that. I couldn't think of another way.

The dressing room backstage was in an uproar. "Has anyone taken my shepherd's crook?" "Hold on, Martha, you've got on too much lipstick." "Miss Campbell, help! Pins are sticking in me!" "Where's my costume? Who's got my costume? I can't find it anywhere. Miss CAMPBELL." "Sheila, are you all right? You sure? You look awfully pale. You're not going to faint, are you?" "No, Miss Campbell, but I've decided I don't want to be in the play." "Nonsense, child." "Miss Campbell, Dave is sitting on my costume, and he won't get up." "What do I do with the star, Miss Campbell?" "Miss Campbell, Gwen was just sick in the corner."

At last everyone was dressed, lipsticked and rouged. We stood offstage waiting for the grade ones to finish singing their carols. I could see my mother with Tom at the end of the first row. The cowlick in Tom's hair glistened under the lights. He wore his best brown corduroy breeches.

The curtain came down in a lopsided way, and the audience started to clap. As soon as the grade ones had filed off, Miss Campbell and Dave Black, the tallest boy in grade two, rushed out to set up the props for our play. The cradle had straw piled all around it, and a cow (two boys with a brown blanket and a false head that looked more like a horse than a cow) stood at one side. On the other side stood a sheep, two girls beneath a sheepskin. The sheep's head, made of cardboard, slipped in an alarming way to the right, as if its neck was broken. Martha, an angel, knelt on one side of the manger. I knelt on the other. Joseph tried to hide behind the sheep.

The curtain rose. A piano began to play "Away In the Manger," the cue for the shepherds to go on stage with their gifts. One shepherd laid his crook in front of the cradle and then turned to leave. But, with the auditorium all in darkness, he missed the exit door and ended up going down the stairs into the audience. The last I saw of him, he was going straight out the fire escape door. I wished it were me.

I heard my cue. I bent over the manger to say my lines. But when I looked down, I saw that the Baby Jesus was really an old doll with a cracked and ugly face, and the words I spoke were loud and hollow in my ears. The lights were blinding, the animals around the manger grotesque. I stumbled off the stage, the applause sounding like dead branches scraping against a window.

Somehow the evening ended. Somehow I got home, the hated costume under my coat. I put it under my clothing in the bottom drawer of the dresser, planning to put it in the garbage can the first chance I got.

I made up the chesterfield in the living room and crawled under the covers, feeling so cold I thought I would never be warm again.

My mother appeared at the living room door, a silhouette against the kitchen light. I started to shiver. "You were very good tonight, Sheila," she said. "I was proud of you."

Now I burned, as if close to a raging fire.

"Where did you get the costume?" I strained to hear if there was any indictment in her voice but heard only warmth, pleasure that I'd done well. I went numb with shame.

"Miss Campbell." I mumbled the words through lips that seemed to be made of rubber.

"I knew that she didn't need to bother us mothers about making costumes," Mom said triumphantly. "What does she have to do when school is finished anyway? She has the rest of the day to herself. If only I were that lucky! Anyway, you looked very nice."

By then I had slid so far down under the covers I could hardly breathe. I wished I'd never heard of plays or speeches or costumes. And I knew it was all over for me. I was headed straight for hell.

seven

On Christmas Eve, Dad arrived home with a small spruce in the back seat of his Ford. "I found it along the river bank near Red Deer," he said. "I have a goose, too. My boss sent it along. His wife's people raise them." The goose, plucked and naked-looking, was taken over by Mom. I helped carry in several mysterious-looking packages that rattled when I shook them.

"Yes, I like it mighty fine there," said Dad. "My boss seems to be satisfied with my work, and Red Deer's a nice little town."

"It's too bad it's so far from home," Mom said, opening cupboard doors, getting down sage, pepper and salt.

Paul and Tom set up the tree in a wooden stand. The box of Christmas decorations was brought up from the basement, and we all helped decorate. Red-and-green crepe paper streamers crisscrossed the ceiling and were hung with tinsel icicles that we'd carefully picked off the Christmas tree last year and saved. Lights glowed among the pungent-smelling spruce branches.

My mother left the room for a minute and came back carrying a brown paper parcel. Removing the paper, she revealed a present that sparkled in its yellow cellophane wrapping and placed it under the tree. "Your Auntie Vera in New York sent you something again, Sheila." I was the only one in our family that Aunt Vera sent a present to. Perhaps it was because I was a girl. Usually it was a dress, a beautiful dress, a dress unlike any dress in our neighbourhood, a dress with a wide skirt that stood straight out when you twirled. As Mrs. Wadleigh said, "A dress with style."

I had presents of my own to set beneath the tree. I'd knitted a scarf for Dad with wool that had been unravelled from an old red sweater. For Mom, I had knitted—this time on a spool and from different colours of wool, like a rainbow—a mat on which to place hot pots. I'd sent away the label from a bag of Sunny Boy Cereal for a picture of Gord Drillon of the Toronto Maple Leafs for Paul. For Tom, I'd made a wind-up car from an empty spool and an elastic band.

Later that night, I became dimly aware that someone was standing in the living room beside where I lay on the chester-field half-asleep. My scalp prickled, and the hairs on my arm stood on end. I knew, without turning my head or opening my eyes, that it was Mom. My whole body went rigid. How long she stood there, I don't know, but it felt like an eternity. I only knew that after a while she left, and I could stop bracing myself for an attack.

In the morning, I wondered if it might have been a night-mare. But when I got up, I saw—on the floor beside the ches-terfield—the hated orange costume.

My mother's voice came whipping at me from the door-way. "I found it when I went into your drawer to get one of your own stockings to hang up, instead of Paul's bigger stocking that you hung for yourself. If the costume belongs to Miss Campbell—as you told me—why is it hidden at the bottom of your drawer?"

I had no words. She came over and began to shake me. "Where did you get it?" she shouted. "Answer me."

My father's quiet voice came from behind me. "I got it for her, Agnes."

Mom's eyes flashed scorn. "This is not store-bought." She scooped up the costume from the floor and flung it at him. "Some woman of yours has made it for her." She sank down into the nearest chair and began to wail, "Oh, isn't it bad enough that you have other women without you dragging your children into it, too? And now Sheila goes behind my back and lies to me on top of it. Oh, merciful Lord in heaven, what have I done to deserve this kind of treatment from the pair of you? You're no good, Frank. It was a black day in heaven the day that I met you."

"Get dressed, Sheila," my father said. I picked up my clothing from the foot of the chesterfield and escaped into the bathroom to dress. My parents were still arguing when I let myself out the back door.

I didn't know where to go, or what to do. It was too early to go calling on anyone in the neighbourhood, especially on Christmas Day. The churches would be open; they were never locked, and there would be a morning Christmas service. But I knew now that I was too bad. The last place I belonged was in a church.

The mountains, floating above a band of silver clouds in the west, seemed to beckon me, and I began to walk in their direction. All I knew was that they were there, and they were beautiful, and I wanted to be near them.

I found myself on a country road standing near a mailbox, barbed wire fences strung on both sides of the road. I thought I must be outside the city limits because there were no longer any signs of streetcar tracks. The wind mourned through the wires of the tall telephone poles.

I saw a farmhouse with a large barn set farther back, and a farm truck parked alongside the house. A dog's barking rang in the cold air. Then I heard a familiar voice call out, "Here, Rex. Come."

A boy was coming from the house to the mailbox where I stood. When he got closer, I saw that it was Dave Black, from school. A collie ran on ahead of him and then bounded over to me.

I bent down to pat the dog, trying to act as if there was nothing unusual about being by myself on a country road on a Christmas morning. "Hi, Dave," I mumbled at last, straightening up.

"Hello." He scuffed his boot back and forth in front of him nervously, turning the snow into ice. "Would you like to see my horse?" he said at last.

I followed him down the narrow road that ran from the highway to his house. As we got close to the two-storey frame house, the door opened, and a woman called out, "Who is your visitor, David?"

We stopped. "This is Sheila Brary, from school," Dave said, introducing us. "I'm going to show her Star."

"I remember you," his mother said, smiling at me. "You were in the Christmas play at school. You made a lovely Mary." I cringed. "Won't you come in first? You must be frozen."

Once inside the warm kitchen, Mrs. Black produced a plate of cinnamon buns and a speckled blue enamel mug of cocoa. She poured herself a cup of tea and joined Dave and me at the oil-clothed table. "This is a treat for me," she said happily. "We have so few visitors." She warmed her hands around her teacup. "I enjoyed the school concert very much. I used to be active in amateur theatre back home in England."

I was surprised and pleased to have Mrs. Black treat me like a grown-up.

The icing on the cinnamon buns was hot and runny. Mom didn't ice her cinnamon buns.

"I do miss it and England. I don't see many people, living out here. There are a couple of old bachelors farming on either side of us, but they seldom visit. That's what I find so hard about Canada, being isolated. Strange, I thought it would be the climate I'd hate. I'd been warned about that, what it would do to my complexion, especially here on the Prairies. But no, it's the loneliness. Back home, our houses were right on the street, and there was always a neighbour popping in to chat."

Though Mrs. Black was much younger than my mother, she was like her in a way I couldn't quite pin down. She talked about how bad the crops had been, about how her husband was determined to stick it out. I studied her. She was fair-haired, my mother's hair was midnight black. Her face was thin, almost gaunt—well, so was Mom's. Mrs. Black's body looked weak and frail. Mom's, in comparison, always looked sturdy to me. But there was worry, loneliness, strain and sadness in Mrs. Black's eyes, brackets encircling the mouth. Just like Mom.

Mr. Black came through the back door with a pail of milk and placed it on the kitchen counter. "Company, is it? That's a right treat for you," he said. "A friend of Dave's? In my day, the boys did the calling." A big man with red cheeks and black hair, he had a hearty laugh.

I found myself relaxing as Mrs. Black talked on about her husband's dream of owning more land. Dad had once said he'd like to run his own business. "Yes, all very well for you men to dream," Mom had said to him then. "As long as you have a woman who'll manage to shuffle up a bit of grub to fill the children's stomachs."

"The land is for David so that he'll have a better life," Mr. Black was saying now. Mrs. Black bent her head and brushed crumbs off the table into her upturned hand.

Dave took me out to the barn to see his horse Star. As soon as we opened the barn door, a heady odour of hay and cow enveloped us. The cows switched their tails and chewed their cuds, moving their jaws from side to side, saliva dropping in long streams from the corners of their mouths. Their eyes followed us as we made our way past the pale pink pig and back to the horses.

In the last stall stood a beautiful chestnut horse with a five-point white blaze on his face. His eyes were so expressive and intelligent that I cried out with delight.

Star hung his head over the top rail and whinnied until Dave rubbed him between the eyes. Dave had brought out a couple of carrots, and he let me feed one to Star. The horse's breath was sweet and warm, his coat sleek under my hand. "I liked Miss Campbell's Christmas story," I told Dave, feeling shy, "the one about the animals in the stable, how they kept the Baby Jesus warm. Do you think it could be true?"

Dave busied himself putting fresh hay in the corner of Star's box, not meeting my eyes. "Yes," he said finally, with a quick warm look at me.

"My mother says that animals talk at midnight on Christmas Eve. Only you can't be there to eavesdrop."

Dave looked dubious at that.

Long after we left the barn, the image of Star's huge eyes remained in my mind.

Mrs. Black insisted I stay for lunch. "It's only potato soup because we're having our big meal tonight, but I can't let you walk all that distance home—and in the cold, too—without something more than a bun in your stomach. Don't worry about getting home. My husband will give you a lift in the truck." The soup was thick and had onions in it. We had canned Saskatoons for dessert.

After I'd helped Mrs. Black with the dishes, she let me set the table for Christmas dinner. "The two bachelors are coming over. I know that they won't say a word all through the meal, but I can't let them heat up a can of beans and call that Christmas dinner."

When the table was set, Mrs. Black frowned and said, "Something's missing…. Napkins. I have some linen ones in my steamer trunk in the bedroom. Come with me and help me look."

The trunk was tucked under the bedroom window, a brown-and-orange crocheted throw draped over it. As I moved past the bed to join Mrs. Black at the trunk, my toe stubbed on the corner of a suitcase stored underneath.

"Oh, my famous suitcase," Mrs. Black said, making a small face. "I keep it packed, ready to go at a moment's notice." Then she laughed. "Well, it helps when things get too difficult."

Did she mean that she would leave? Leave Dave? Would mothers do that?"It might be different if I had a daughter," she went on. "I find it so dreary with just men around. They're all right, in their own way, but they're not enough. Maybe it's because I grew up in a house full of girls. There were seven of us. Females are so much more interesting, don't you think?"

I didn't know how to answer that.

~

"You don't care how much grief you cause me, Sheila," my mother said, winding up her long list of complaints. She turned back to the stove and stirred the gravy. The goose glistened brown in the warming oven.

"I'm so sorry, Mom," I whispered.

"Yes, well, sorry doesn't mend anything, does it?"

"No." I stared at the jar of goose grease she'd poured off. I knew it would be used to rub on our chests when we had coughs.

"I've a good mind to make you go without Christmas dinner. After what you and your no-good father have done to me.

Cheating. Deceit. Lies. It's a good thing you weren't around today, or I would have taken the strap to you."

Around and around went her spoon. The gravy thickened, bubbled gently. A smell of onion and sage and browned goose skin filled the kitchen. I heard a flurry of small pops from the living room. Tom must have got a cap gun for Christmas.

After a few minutes, she said, "Don't you even want to see what your Auntie Vera sent you from New York?"

"All right." I walked listlessly into the living room and opened the present slowly. I felt as if I were dying. Nothing seemed to matter anymore.

A jumper of blue cloth and a white blouse of the same fabric lay folded neatly inside. Red rickrack trimmed the bottom of the skirt. No one at school had anything like it.

"Why don't you try them on, Sheila," my father said from the easy chair where he sat reading.

"No. Not now."

"And you haven't seen what I got for you."

"I have to go help Mom with dinner," I said quickly, not looking at him.

"Sheila," he said. He sounded disappointed, and I wanted to cry.

He got up, went over to the tree and handed me a small present, about the size of a jewellery box. Maybe it was a locket. I had said I wanted one.

"To you from me with love," he said. My throat ached with what I wanted to say and couldn't. At that instant, out of the corner of my eye, I caught a glimpse of my mother at the door. Her face was hard and disapproving. Her eyes darted first to Dad, then to me.

I placed Dad's unopened present on the arm of the easy chair. "Thank you," I said and turned away from him to join my mother in the doorway.

I chanced one brief look back at Dad. He was staring at me, an expression of hurt in his eyes. As I turned to go into the kitchen, I saw Mom smile at Dad. It was a cruel smile, and her eyes above it glittered with triumph.

By the time Christmas Day ended, my shoulders ached. I knew I'd been holding them up around my ears, as if ready to ward off any attack from my mother.

I dropped into bed, pulled up the covers and turned on my side to sleep. Minutes later, the covers were jerked roughly from my face. My mother's voice was ugly as she asked, "Did you have a nice Christmas, Sheila?" I lay very still. Whatever I said would be wrong. "Because *I* didn't. Thanks to you and your father." She yanked the covers up so that now they covered my head. But I could still hear her voice. "I want you to know that I hate both you and your father."

I could hardly breathe, but I waited until I heard Mom's footsteps leave the room before I cautiously put my head up from beneath the covers. I could see Mom's shadow pass back and forth in the kitchen. Dad was there, too, I could smell his cigarette smoke.

Tears came rolling silently down into my mouth, tasting salty. It took me a long time to fall asleep, until I thought of Dave's horse, and the memory of Star's dark, liquid eyes came shining through the dark to comfort me.

After breakfast the next morning, Dad hauled his suitcase out to the car to drive back to Red Deer. The weather had turned colder during the night, and snow fell heavily. There were frost patterns on the inside of the windows.

"You will send money home, Frank?" Mom asked anxiously. "And regularly? You know that the city won't issue me a relief cheque now that you're working."

Dad sounded weary. "Yes, Agnes, I'll send money home."

"I'm going to rent out the dining room again. Every little bit of cash helps."

"Yes, Agnes, you do that." He sounded as if he would agree with her no matter what she said.

Before Dad left, he came over to the front window where I'd melted a peephole in the frost with my thumb. "I want to talk to you, Snooks," he said. Usually that nickname made me feel warm inside, but now I steeled myself against it and against Dad.

My father put his arm around my shoulders. "You're too young to understand what's going on between your mother and me," he said gently. "But it's important that you don't blame yourself. These things have no bearing on you. Certainly not on the kind of person that you are."

I was petrified that Mom would come in and see us talking together. Didn't he know how hard he was making it for me? My breath came quickly. I was almost panting with anxiety.

"Honey," Dad pleaded. "Don't turn away from me this way."

I looked in the direction of the kitchen and saw Mom stop her work there and move to its doorway. I shook myself free from Dad's arm.

"Sheila!" he said, looking and sounding shocked.

"Leave me alone!" I said loud enough for Mom to be sure to hear.

"Oh, Sheila," Dad said sadly. "This is not you! And it isn't good for you to make yourself behave this way." He shook his head, as if in disbelief. I backed away, my heart closed tight against him.

But I had made up my mind. There was nothing else I could do but turn against him, not if I was going to survive in the same house with my mother.

eight

In the days that followed, I stayed out of the house as much as possible. I visited Martha and the neighbours, went to Sunday School, anywhere that would keep me out from under Mom's critical eye.

Every chance she got, my mother quizzed me. "Who is the woman who made that costume? What does she look like? Do you think your father has known her for a long time? Is she younger than I am? Prettier?"

"I don't know," I answered, feeling miserable. "I told you. I don't know."

School was my refuge. Though I wasn't doing as well as I had. Miss Campbell asked me to see her after school. "Your last three art assignments are long overdue, and here it is, almost Easter time," she said.

"They didn't turn out very well. I'm redoing them."

"Let me see them, please."

I gave her my art portfolio.

"There's nothing wrong with these, Sheila. They're perfectly all right. Now show me the ones you're doing to replace them."

I handed her the first one, which was only partially done.

"You're doing a very careful job—I can see that—but it isn't really necessary to be that exacting. Why do you make extra work for yourself?"

"I don't know."

"Don't be afraid to make mistakes. It's much better to hand in your work on time and get a B-plus than to hand it in late, trying to get an A." Miss Campbell's kindness made me feel like weeping. "Your work is commendable as it is. There's no need to try to be perfect." She picked up my first efforts again and singled one out. "Now, this watercolour…I like it very much. It's a pineapple weed, isn't it?

"I don't know—I guess it does smell like a pineapple. All I know is that it grows behind our house and down at the slough. There's a farm down near the slough, and the farmer there says that his turkeys like to eat it, so he calls it turkey weed."

I didn't tell Miss Campbell that on my gloomiest days— when nothing I did seemed to please Mom, no matter how hard I tried—the sight of the turkey weed's yellow buds and green, ferny leaves and its slightly astringent scent lifted my heart, giving me hope.

Miss Campbell glanced quickly through my late assignments, the ones I hadn't turned in. "Let me keep these," she said with an encouraging smile. "You do seem to be very fond of one colour scheme, the split-complementary red, violet and yellow-green. Can we look at the colour wheel and work out another colour scheme?" She put her finger on the blue segment of the colour wheel, then moved to the secondary colour beside it, green, and then across to their two opposites, red-orange. "Do you see, Sheila, that by moving just one step to the side, you can create a new colour scheme?" Miss Campbell leaned towards me with a serious face and said, "It's very much like that in many things. They are really marginal. If we could move one step to the side, we would see things differently." She paused, her eyebrows little tents of earnestness. "Do you understand—even a little—what I'm trying to say to you?"

"I...think so." But I didn't, really. *Marginal. Move one step away.* All I could do was store it away in my mind until I could make sense of it.

Her voice softened. "Your mother was in to see me," she said. "I was sorry to hear about the trouble the costume caused."

I felt as if I had fallen into the icy slush.

"Sheila, I want you to know that if, in the future you have any problem, you can come to me. We can always work out something so that no one is hurt.... Are you all right? You're very pale."

I couldn't speak.

At that moment, Martha stuck her head in the door. "Oh, sorry. I'm looking for Sheila. We're supposed to go to Brownies."

"Run along then, Sheila," said Miss Campbell.

As Martha and I clattered down the stairs, she said, "They're going to be talking about summer camp today, even though it's a long way away. I really want to go, but Grandma's worried about my asthma."

"Asthma? What's that?"

"You know that wheeze I get sometimes? That's asthma."

"Oh." Was that why her grandmother took such good care of her, always giving her vitamins and cod liver oil and tonics? The only health measure we took in our house was to make sure not to sleep with our feet to the north. Mom said that the North Pole's magnet drew our strength out through the soles of our feet. Most beds in our house faced east to west, which made for some peculiar arrangements of furniture. The chesterfield I slept on lay north to south, but I slept with my feet pointing south. None of us had asthma. Should I mention this to Martha's grandmother?

We crossed kitty-corner from the school to the United Church where the Brownies met. I'd been about to give up Brownies. The strain of being good in yet one more place was getting to be too much.

Like yesterday, at school. Dave Black had grabbed me amid the soggy coats in the cloakroom and tried to kiss me. Even though I'd liked it, I pushed him away and kicked him in the shins. Then I'd gone into the classroom and told Gwen Mainwaring that she wasn't supposed to chew gum in school. Later on after school, when I couldn't find one overshoe, I'd sworn. "Damn! Damn! Damn!"

"You are going from bad to worse." Mom had summed it up when I yelled at Tom at home. "I don't know what I'm going to do with you."

One morning as I was leaving for school, Mom said, "I've made an appointment for you to see Father Kelly at four-thirty today. You are to go there straight after school and no dilly-dallying. You do remember where St. Joseph's is? It's been so long since you set foot in the Catholic Church, I wouldn't wonder if you'd forgotten."

What would Dad say? He'd laid down the law. We children were not to go inside the Catholic Church.

It was as if Mom had read my mind. "What does it matter what your father says? He hasn't been home since Christmas, and I have no idea when he'll turn up. I wonder sometimes if we'll ever see him again." The dark circles around my mother's eyes made her look as if she'd been punched with the streetcar conductor's ticket puncher. "Maybe Father Kelly can help you. Otherwise, at the rate you're going, you'll end up in the reform school."

All the way to St. Joseph's after school, I wondered what Father Kelly would say. My feet dragged as I turned in at the church's black, wrought iron gate. An arrow directed me around the side to the office. Once there, I pulled a bell on a chain and heard an answering chime deep inside.

The door opened abruptly, and a woman stood there in a black dress with a white apron over it, hair skewered so tightly behind her head that her skin seemed stretched. "Are you the Brary child?" she demanded.

"Yes."

She stepped aside. "Wipe your feet. I don't want snow tracked in here."

The hall gleamed with wax, and a narrow, maroon-coloured rug ran the length of it. I wiped my feet carefully and followed behind the housekeeper. She knocked softly at the door at the end of the hall.

"Come in," said a voice that sounded kinder than I'd anticipated. My hands, which were tight fists, loosened a little. The woman opened the door.

"Oh, yes," said Father Kelly, making a move as if to get up but never quite completing it. He waved me to a seat opposite him and sank back into the swivel chair behind his desk. "You could make us a cup of hot chocolate, if you would be so kind, Mrs. Connors," he said. The woman, hovering at the doorway, pursed her lips.

"Just shut that door behind you, Mrs. Connors.... Now... Sheila, is it?" he said, consulting a note on his desk. "Yes, Sheila Brary." He leaned back. "And how is your mother keeping these days? I haven't seen her for a long time." Without waiting for my answer, he went on, "You have a number of brothers, I seem to recall. You're the only girl. Not fair at times, is it?"

I opened my mouth to speak.

"Now your mother seems to be worried about you. Why is that, do you think? She says something about your father being a bad influence on you. Something about you getting into trouble with him. Or because of him? I couldn't quite get the straight of that."

My mouth was so dry, my lips stuck together. I concentrated on sitting up straight and not scuffing my feet on the rug. The clock on the wall suddenly made a whirring sound, startling me.

"Is your father at home now?"

"No, Father Kelly."

"When was he home last?"

"Christmas time, Father Kelly."

"And there was something that happened…something about a Christmas play and a costume? Something that upset your mother a great deal?"

I stared at the picture of Christ on the wall opposite. He was praying in a garden, and he had drops of blood like perspiration on his forehead.

Father Kelly reached for a pipe that lay on an ashtray on the corner of his desk. He made elaborate preparations before finally lighting it. From time to time, his eyes would lift from his pipe to study me.

Mrs. Connors slid silently into the room with two cups of hot chocolate on a tray. As the warm liquid eased down my throat, I began to feel better.

Father Kelly smoked away. The smell of the tobacco in the air was sweet as apples.

"I know your father, Sheila, I have for years." Father Kelly knocked his pipe on the edge of the ashtray. "I like the man. It's hard not to."

I was so surprised, I set my cup down with a clatter in its saucer.

"Everybody likes your father," Father Kelly said. He leaned forward. "He's the life of the party wherever he goes. Plays a fine fiddle, too. Did you know that? Used to play for all the dances in Medicine Hat when he lived there. A grand sort of man. But not a marrying kind of man." Then hastily, "Not that you would know what I mean, but let's just say that it's hard for him to settle down. Your mother now…. Well, she's a fine, decent hard-working woman. No finer woman. Her life is not an easy one, God knows. She's having to be both mother and father to you children, and in these hard times, too. It's not the way the good Lord intended it to be, not at all. In short, Sheila, my dear child, you must try to be as kind to her as possible."

I stared at the pattern on the rug, a geometric design in varying shades of green.

"Would you try to do that?" he asked.

I shifted my eyes to his feet, which were visible under his desk. Polished black oxfords, about the same size as my father's, which would make them a size ten.

"Eh, my girl?"

"I do try, Father, as hard as I can. But it's no use. I can't seem to do anything right. Ever." I swallowed a couple of times and kept my eyes on Father Kelly's shoes.

He got up from behind his desk and went over to the window, staring out. With the coming dusk, the sky was beginning to turn purple. Father Kelly just stood there, hands clasped behind his back, swaying back and forth.

Back and forth. It was soothing to watch him, like swinging on a swing. From somewhere, the sound of a piano came drifting down the hallway and into the room. I sat listening to the music, and it and the purple dusk seemed to be the only things real.

Father Kelly started to talk in a low voice—as if to himself—still staring out the window. "They will do as they please. They won't come to church. There's no sign of them from one year's end to the next. Then when there's trouble—oh, yes, when it's too late—then they come, and I'm supposed to perform some kind of miracle. Fix everything. What else do these poor souls expect but trouble?"

Mrs. Connors came tapping at the door. "You have another visitor waiting, Father."

Father Kelly turned from the window. His eyes looked sad. In a tired voice he said, "Tell your mother that I did speak to you as she requested, Sheila. Maybe she'll…. In the meantime, try to understand and be kind to her. There's a good girl."

"But I am not a good girl."

"You could be. Try to think of all the wonderful qualities your mother has and keep your thoughts fastened there."

Outside, the setting sun was painting bands of rose and mauve behind the mountains. I wondered what Dad was doing right then. Was he surrounded by friends, the life of the party, ready to play his fiddle for their dancing? You could warm your hands at the life in Dad. And I wanted to be like him. But I had to live with Mom, and I had to survive, and now I had orders to be kind to her. It seemed impossible.

The dark came down from the sky like a blanket, and all of a sudden it was bitterly cold. I bent my head and turned in the direction of home.

CHAPTER
nine

I asked my mother if I could have a party.

"But your birthday isn't until September."

"Yes, September first. School hasn't even started by then. And I've already been to three birthday parties this year. It's my turn to give one."

To my delight, she agreed, even though I'd heard her tell Mrs. Bruce next door, "I'm not sleeping well at night, what with the baby due in six weeks and all."

But now she was saying, "You can invite six children. I'll have to do some stretching to give them anything to eat."

"Like what would you give them?"

"Jam sandwiches and cocoa. A plain cake."

I invited three boys and three girls, including Martha, Dave Black and Arthur Cool who sat behind me at school. Arthur had given me my biggest valentine, a red tinfoil heart on a paper doily and on it had printed, "*I love you.*" I'd given him my best valentine in return.

Arthur wore round-necked sweaters and tan corduroy breeches. His hair was slicked down with an even parting on the left side. I'd been to his birthday party. There were balloons and favours and a store-bought cake with fluffy icing that left a cloying taste in my mouth. Arthur was an only child, and his mother never left the room except to fetch more food.

On the day of the party, I proudly led my five guests home after school. Martha had a chest cold and couldn't come. I was bubbling with excitement. These were my friends, and we were going to play Blind-Man's Bluff and Pin-the-Tail-on-the-Donkey. As we got close to my house, I saw Arthur's eyes scrutinize our picket fence. It needed painting and was missing several pickets. Other places had been mended with unpainted laths.

Arthur's voice went high with disbelief. "You live here?"

"Yes, I told you I lived only a block from school."

When we went through the front door, Arthur stared at the shabby, worn furniture, a look of disdain wrinkling his face. Later, I noticed that he only ate one sandwich—leaving the crust, something my mother did not allow us to do—took one look at his cup of cocoa and set the cup down.

"What's the matter?" I asked. "Don't you like cocoa?"

"Not with a skin on the top."

I took a teaspoon and removed the offending skin, putting it on my own saucer. "My mom boils the cocoa," I explained. "It's not good for your stomach if you don't." He was not impressed.

The next two hours limped by. Mentally, I began to urge everyone to go home, go home. They hadn't seemed to notice that my mother had washed and waxed the kitchen floor, worn as it was. They couldn't know, of course, that she was wearing her best dress—the sea-green crepe that she wore to Social

Credit meetings—and that the Cuban-heel pumps with the straps across her insteps were cutting into her swollen feet. She had spent time on her hair. All this she had done for them.

When Arthur left, he politely thanked my mother for the party. I walked with him to the door. "I never knew you were poor," he said, and the words fell like stones into my heart.

I was stunned. We had food. My mother was a good cook. She had given the best party she could.

What did he mean, poor? I didn't feel poor. I followed him out onto the sidewalk and grabbed his arm. "I'm not poor," I said. "We had a cow once. I know how to play the piano. And I've got three brothers already." I shook his arm. "Three brothers," I emphasized. "And maybe another one in a month."

I watched him hurry away down the street. No valentine for him next year.

~

It was a week later that the milkman noticed that old Mr. Green's milk bottles had not been taken in from the previous day. The milkman went to Mr. Green's living room window and looked in. Then he went to the next-door-neighbour and called the police.

By the time the ambulance arrived, the whole neighbourhood was out in the street in front of Mr. Green's. Two uniformed young men carried in an empty stretcher and came out with the body of Bill Green covered with a grey blanket. There were hushed murmurs, and I heard the words "suicide" and "hung himself." I was shocked. Sometimes, when Mom had been in a bad mood for days and days, she would say she wished she were dead, but for someone to actually *do* it....

At home, Mom wouldn't let us talk about Bill Green's suicide, other than, "It's not for us to judge. Not one of us knows what another soul is suffering."

But everyone else in the neighbourhood *did* talk about Mr. Green's suicide. Even at the United Church during the sermon, the minister said that if a certain man—and he wasn't mentioning any names—had been religious, he would not have committed suicide. "No, brothers and sisters in Christ, he would have known that God was ever nigh. 'They that wait upon the Lord shall renew their strength; they shall mount up with wings as eagles; they shall run, and not be weary; and they shall walk and not faint.'"

I tried to talk to my mother about this. I knew she was religious, yet I often saw her in despair. But all she could say was, "I'm sure, that at our end, God will have mercy on all of us." Then, to herself more than to me, "Otherwise, where would be the sense in all of it?"

For the next couple of weeks, I talked Martha into walking down the lane behind Bill Green's house and peeking in through the fence at his empty house. With the blinds pulled halfway down, the house looked lonely. I couldn't help wondering what Bill Green was thinking about when he did it, hung the rope, put the noose around his neck. Just how unhappy did grown-ups have to be before they did this unbelievable act?

~

The end of March brought wild crocuses to the southern slopes of the foothills behind our house. With their delicate mauve cups and silver hairs on fragile stems, they had the faintest of fragrances. The meadowlarks, too, were back, spilling their five-note golden song over the slopes in an almost unbearable sweetness. I gathered a bunch of the flowers to take to my mother. She loved crocuses.

One late afternoon, the bigger boys climbed the water tower that sat behind the school and was inside a chain fence clearly marked "KEEP OUT." Their shouts from above sounded free and exhilarated, and I scaled the chain fence and started up after them. Halfway up, I paused to look down at the countryside spread out before me and felt an overwhelming longing to fly far away and never come back. Maybe this was the way the canary in our classroom at school felt when people poked their fingers into the cage, making it skitter to one side. I wanted to fly away and sing the song that seemed to be stuck like a bone in my throat. A longing for Dad flooded over me, and with the prairie wind lifting my hair, I looked north to where the highway ran to Red Deer and willed him to come home and rescue me. Then the sun began to set, and I heard the bigger boys coming down.

Once back on the ground at the foot of the tower and outside the protective fencing, I knew it wouldn't matter if Dad did come home. I would have to pretend I was no longer his "little girl" because I'd already aligned myself with Mom against him.

Walking back home, I began to daydream. What if I got enough Brownie badges to go to camp? What if I wrote Dad, and he came to visit me at camp at Sylvan Lake? Red Deer wasn't that far away, according to the map. What if….

I was home. The passageway that ran by the next-door neighbour's house, the Bruces, had never seemed so long. I saw Mrs. Bruce dusting her bedroom dresser when I went by her window, and I quickly turned my eyes away in case she thought I was being nosey. "One thing I can't abide," my mother always said, "are people who are nosey."

My brother Mark was born at home at seven o'clock in the morning on Easter Sunday with the nurse from the Victorian Order of Nurses there to help. A skinny baby, he didn't cry until the nurse held him up by his heels and slapped his bottom, and even then, the cry was feeble.

My mother's voice was weak. "It's no wonder he isn't strong," she said as she held out her arms for him, "with barely enough food in the house to keep us alive. He feels so cold." She opened her gown and held him close to her breast, folding the bedclothes so that he was covered snugly, but his face open to the air.

"Who's going to help you out for the next couple of weeks?" asked the nurse, concern in her voice. "Where is your husband?"

Mom turned her head away, but not before I saw the look of shame in her eyes. "I thought he would surely be here by now," she said.

"Is there a relative, a close friend, you could call in?"

"No."

"The neighbours, then," the nurse suggested.

"I don't want to bother them. Sheila can stay home from school and give me a hand."

The nurse's voice was firm. "Sheila belongs in school. And with this sickly baby, you'll need an adult's help. There has to be someone."

"How about Mrs. Powers?" I piped from the doorway where I had been hovering during most of the procedure. I knew that Mom didn't like the neighbours to know too much about our business, but somehow Mrs. Powers was different.

The nurse began to remove the soiled newspapers from under Mom. "Do you mean the Mrs. Powers from Olds who used to room here and who lost her husband to TB?" She thought for a moment. "I think that's a good idea. How could I reach her, Mrs. Brary?"

"Sheila, fetch the latest letter from Mrs. Powers. It's tucked behind the kitchen clock."

"I'll phone Mrs. Powers and see what we can arrange." The nurse's voice became more cheerful. "Now turn on your other side, Mrs. Brary, so that I can tuck this clean pad under you."

Before leaving, the nurse checked the baby again. She wiped away the mucous that had gathered at his mouth and flicked his purple feet until a faint blush appeared under the skin. "I'll be in to see you and the baby again this afternoon," she promised Mom, pulling on her leather gloves and adjusting her neat, blue V.O.N. hat. "In the meantime, try to get as much rest as you can."

When the nurse returned shortly after lunch, she reported that Mrs. Powers was unable to come. "The V.O.N. nurse in Olds said that Mrs. Powers is sick in bed with pneumonia. I'll be in to see you twice a day, Mrs. Brary. Your neighbour next-door says she'll bring in your meals until you're stronger."

Mom began to sit up in protest. The nurse eased her back. "I'll try to get in touch with your husband."

Mrs. Bruce was as good as her word. Later that day, she brought over a pot of beef-and-barley stew, plus a loaf of freshly baked bread, a dozen cinnamon buns, a tin of oatmeal cookies and a large bowl of custard.

"I have several bottles of stout at the house that would do you the world of good," she said to Mom. "The women back home in the Old Country swear it brings in the milk."

"No," said Mom firmly. "I took an oath of temperance in Ireland when I was twenty-one, and I've never let a drop of liquor pass my lips."

Mrs. Bruce's mouth turned down in dismay. "Drink was a problem in Glasgow, too—I'll admit that—but it's not the same here in Canada. You're going to need all the nourishment you can get. How is the wee babe? I haven't heard a peep from him."

Mom folded back the shawl Mark was wrapped in. His face was white and wizened-looking.

"You must let me send over the stout," Mrs. Bruce insisted. "It's full of all these vitamins they're talking about. Whatever did we do before we knew about them? Please, Mrs. Brary. Think of it as medicine for the bairn." Mom didn't answer. She looked so pale, so tired. "There, there," Mrs. Bruce said, "I'm talking too much and wearing you out."

Over the next few days, the whole neighbourhood came in with a small gift for the baby—a blanket, a pair of knitted booties, food. We were eating better than we had for a long time. The baby slept most of the time. He would only nurse a few minutes before falling back to sleep, and no matter what Mom did, she couldn't wake him up again.

Strain grew in Mom's face, and she began to complain that her left ear ached. One night she cried out sharply with the pain, and I heard her get up and stumble into the pantry. Then I heard the oven door open. There was the sharp smell of gas. I sat up, my heart banging against my ribs. *Oh, no. Oh, God, don't let her kill herself. Not like Bill Green.* Then there was the reassuring *poof* as the flame caught, and after a while an onion smell wafted into the living room. A few minutes later, I got up and went into the kitchen.

Mom was taking a roasted onion from the oven. She dropped it into one of my brother's woollen socks and went back to bed with the sock held up to her ear.

In the morning, she could barely drag herself out of bed. She began to make the porridge, but she was crying all the time, sharp little cries of pain, as she pressed her hand to her ear.

I ran next door to the Bruces. Mr. Bruce phoned his doctor. "Never mind," I heard Mr. Bruce say. "I'll pay the bill. Just come."

"I'm worried about mastoiditis," the doctor told the Bruces after examining Mom. "By rights, she belongs in the hospital." I saw his eyes take in the cracked linoleum, the diapers strung on a line running from above the kitchen sink to the water heater, my brothers and me in our assorted nightwear of old shirts and sweaters. "Her husband will have to be found." He shook his head. "This is surely one of the saddest cases I've ever seen. As for the baby…." He paused. "I don't give it much of a chance unless it's bottle-fed every three hours right around the clock."

"The neighbours are here to help," said Mrs. Bruce.

"She can't fight the infection unless she gets her proper rest. Could you find out the husband's last address? I'll send him a telegram."

He left a bottle containing a vile-looking, green medicine. "Give her two teaspoons every four hours," he instructed Mrs. Bruce. The doctor went on about ear drops and hot water bottles and plenty of rest and fluids.

Days went by, but there still was no sign of Dad. Mr. Bruce's face grew dark and angry, and Mrs. Bruce was forever shushing him up. Apparently, Dad had lost his Red Deer job, and the Mounties were trying to track down his whereabouts.

Under the care of the neighbours, the house was clean. There was food on the table, and the baby was taking an ounce or two of formula made with canned milk, water and corn syrup.

I still heard Mom crying every night. Even with the neighbourhood women's help and their casseroles. In spite of the doctor's medicine.

Terror grew in me. *Dad just has to come home.*

CHAPTER
ten

"I won't go to the hospital unless my husband is here to look after the children," Mom said to the doctor when he visited the next day. Nothing he could say would change her mind.

The Mounties finally located Dad. He had started a new job as a salesman based in Edmonton, selling lilac trees and honeysuckle to farmers' wives. He returned to Calgary in a new grey Ford and parked it with a flourish outside our house, then came up the front sidewalk. He wore his hat at a jaunty angle, and he didn't look the least bit concerned, as far as I could see.

As soon as Dad walked into the bedroom, Mom cried out with a sound of relief. Her face softened and lost its haunted look. Dad sank down on the edge of the bed and put his arms around her. She cried into his shoulder.

"I didn't have a minute to write," he said. "All I knew was that I had to hustle around to get another job. Owed that much to you and our little family. I didn't have the heart to write and tell you of all the troubles I was having, knowing that you had your hands full here at home with the kiddies."

He looked down at the baby sleeping beside Mom. "Another boy. We seem to have a run on them in this family, don't we?" He straightened the top sheet so that it lay smooth around her. "Now I want you to forget everything and leave it all to me. The doctor wants you to go into the hospital…no, you're not to worry for a minute about the bills. We'll cross that bridge when we come to it."

While Mom dressed and packed a small bag for the hospital, Dad heated up some soup for lunch. Then he helped Mom into the black seal coat he'd bought her before the Depression began. We all drove to the hospital with Mom. I was crunched in the back seat with Paul and Tom; Andy stood between my legs. The baby slept in a small basket at Mom's feet.

The thought of Mom going away from us filled me with anguish. Everywhere I looked was grey. The interior of the car. Grey houses on the street. Grey street. Even the hospital, when we got there, was made of huge grey stones, like a forbidding fortress.

I kept my hand pressed against my mouth to keep from crying out as I watched Dad walk Mom slowly up the steps to the front entrance. I was so afraid I'd never see Mom again that I flung open the back door of the car and ran after her.

"Mom!" I screamed, just as she was disappearing into the doorway. She stopped, turned and waited for me. When I reached her, she bent down and touched my face.

"Sheila, try not to worry. I'll be back. You must be brave for the boys' sake. I'm counting on you to take care of them for me." Then she turned back to the cavernous doors and disappeared.

Dad had no sooner driven away from the hospital than he turned the car around and pointed it in the direction of downtown. Soon we were pulling up in front of a house that looked too familiar. Irene's.

"Wait in the car," Dad told us as he straightened his tie and smoothed back his hair. He fished in his vest pocket for his package of Sen-Sen and shook a couple into his mouth. "Now behave yourselves until I get back," he said. "I don't want my new car scratched in any way."

Heartsick, I huddled in the back seat. Paul stared glumly out the window. Tom took out his jackknife and a piece of wood and started whittling away. Andy was getting restless, and I took him for a short walk up and down the street.

It seemed to be forever before Dad reappeared. Irene was with him, carrying a scuffed suitcase that banged against her knees. Dad opened the front door for her, and she slid in, narrowly missing baby Mark in his basket on the floor. Irene rearranged her clothing, giving Dad a sidelong glance. Then she twisted around to smile at me. I shrank down, unable to smile back.

"Irene's going to stay with us while your mother's in the hospital," Dad said, turning the ignition key. "So I want you all to be nice to her and help her as much as you can. She doesn't have to help out like this, you know, but that's the kind of person she is." He looked over at her with a satisfied smile. His lips suddenly seemed swollen. I slouched further down in the seat.

None of us children said a word all the way home. Dad and Irene laughed and chatted as if they were going on a picnic. Once home, Dad put Irene's suitcase in the front bedroom.

I went to bed early that night. I couldn't bear to see or hear what was going on around me.

Irene wore a satin housecoat to breakfast, a pale pink, the same colour as the pig I'd seen on Dave Black's farm. The housecoat gaped at the top and revealed breasts that looked empty at the top and then sagged right out of sight. I wondered how she managed to make them look so full and pointy when she wore a sweater. I felt contempt for my father that he would prefer Irene to Mom.

Irene drank three cups of tea at breakfast and smoked a cigarette with each one. Grey ash piled up in her saucer, and I raised my eyes from it to look at the poplar tree that grew outside our kitchen window. Its new yellow-green leaves glistened and spun in the morning sunlight.

By the time we came home from school, Irene had changed into a skirt and sweater. The sweater was stained and matted under the arms, and she smelled stale, like a musty drawer. My mother always smelled of newly washed clothes that had been hung outside in the fresh air. She hung them even in the wintertime, and they froze on the clothesline, looking like a row of people at attention.

Irene knew only one way to cook and that was to fry: eggs, sausages, bacon, hash browns, pan toast, pork chops, pancakes. Vegetables and fruit disappeared. The only one who got any milk was the baby.

Irene had the radio on all the time. *Ma Perkins, The Guiding Light, The Major Bowes Hour,* anything, as long as it was noise.

Unwashed clothing began to pile up on top of the washing machine in the bathroom. If I needed a pair of underwear pants, I learned to rummage through the dirty laundry to find the least dirty pair. Dishes—whenever Irene washed them—were rinsed quickly under the cold-water tap and left to dry on the drain board. The wood of the drain board soon became slimy and sour-smelling. Mom always said about us, "We may be poor, but we're clean." Now we lived in squalor.

I hated being home, but when I was out of the house, I was always afraid that something bad might happen if I wasn't there to stop it. After all, Mom had told me to take care of the boys.

Dad had a new job selling spices and flavourings for Watkins. He carried a display case lined in grey felt. It contained tins of pepper, sage, thyme, cinnamon and nutmeg, and bottles of vanilla, almond and lemon extract. All these were held in place with narrow bands made of an elastic, blue, silky fabric. I sniffed at all the tops of the tins and bottles, catching whiffs of exotic, foreign lands. One day, I promised myself, I would escape from this house and go there.

Irene occasionally did alterations for Eaton's. Then, her foot on the pedal, Irene would make her sewing machine *whir* in the living room, while in the background, the radio blared even louder.

Irene did not get excited easily. Even if Mark screamed and got red in the face, Irene just said to me, "Don't be such a worry wart. He'll be all right."

Dad went to see Mom every couple of days, taking a can of pineapple juice with him. "It's the only thing she can keep down," he said. "She's running a fever and is delirious most of the time."

One night after I'd gone to bed on the chesterfield in the living room, I heard Irene say to Dad, "It's not as if she's ever been, well, normal. We'd all probably be better off if she were to…." She had dropped her voice, and I couldn't hear the rest. But I lay rigid with fear and stared through the darkness around me.

Weeks passed, and still Mom stayed in the hospital. I tried to keep away from home and Irene as much as possible, even though I *was* supposed to watch out for my brothers. After school, I offered to clean blackboards, sharpen pencils and water plants. That done, I'd work on my scrapbook, a book of house plans. I had started with the kitchen, choosing an Armstrong ad from the *Ladies' Home Journal.* Everything was there for a happy family: red-brick floor linoleum, white gleaming stove, a pine table with matching chairs. Around four-thirty, Miss Campbell would look up from the papers she was marking. "Time to go home now," she'd say.

My feet would begin to drag as soon as I stepped on the sidewalk of our street. Bill Green's house still remained empty, and its windows stared at me, bleak as death. Sometimes I would visit Mrs. Wadleigh, across the field. As soon as I stepped into the Wadleighs'—with its fresh smell, shiny hardwood floors and tidy kitchen—Bill Green's suicide would slide from my mind.

Mrs. Wadleigh was helping me with my Brownie badges. I was still hoping to get to Brownie camp, and I had now earned badges for knitting, darning and cooking and was working on the crochet badge.

Some days after I left the Wadleighs, I went down to the slough that lay at the foot of the hills behind our house. There I looked for violets and shooting stars. In the spilling golden light, kneeling on the spongy hillocks and looking at the brown water that gradually seeped into a small, clear stream, I began to feel more peaceful. Then I would lift my head, see spring pulsing all around, and would begin to believe again that Mom would get better and come back home to us.

One school morning after we'd recited the Lord's Prayer, Miss Campbell chose the twenty-third psalm for the Bible reading. It was the first time I'd heard it, and the beauty of the words flooded through me, as if I'd stepped from a dark place into dazzling sunlight.

Later that same day, Miss Campbell handed out mimeographed copies of the psalm with type that was fat and mauve.

"I want you to memorize this," she said. "It is one of the most beautiful poems in the world." I handled the page, as if it were a treasure.

After school, I went out to the foothills behind our house. I went to a favourite spot, a little valley between two rounded hills that looked comfortable as breasts. I lay on my back. Overhead, the sky was a singing-kind of blue.

I turned on my side, my face resting on the dead prairie wool. But I smelled the freshness of new grass and saw green blades pushing their way through the old stubble. Gradually, I felt a great calm come over me, a reassurance that, in spite of winter storms, harsh winds and plummeting temperatures, spring came again in a well-appointed universe.

The words of the psalm had been in my mind all day. Each sentence was full of wonders. I murmured the words from memory.

The Lord is my shepherd; I shall not want.

He maketh me to lie down in green pastures: he leadeth me beside the still waters,

He restoreth my soul: he leadeth me in the paths of righteousness for his name's sake.

Yea, though I walk through the valley of the shadow of death, I will fear no evil: for thou art with me: thy rod and thy staff they comfort me.

Thou preparest a table before me in the presence of mine enemies: thou anointest my head with oil; my cup runneth over.

Surely goodness and mercy shall follow me all the days of my life: and I will dwell in the house of the Lord forever.

It was easy to imagine a shepherd up on the brow of the hill. Water glinted at the bottom of the valley, and sheep bleated from the farm near the slough.

I was inside the psalm and stayed there until the sun had disappeared, and the air grew chill. It was the first time I knew the healing power of words.

At home, I'd catch Paul studying Dad and Irene. If Paul noticed me watching him, he'd glance quickly away. As for Tom, he had developed a passion for carving and had confiscated a corner in the basement. "It's mine," he declared.

Mark, the baby, continued to feed only half-heartedly. Instead of trying to waken him, as Mom had done when he stopped sucking the offered bottle, Irene laid him back on the bed and picked up a cigarette. Once I tried to coax another ounce of formula into him, and Irene had squinted at me through cigarette smoke as if I were demented.

One day Andy fell from his high chair. At least that's what Dad told us when we asked about the large, purple bump on the side of Andy's forehead. "It happened after you kiddies left for school this morning," he explained. "But don't tell your mother—there's no need to worry her." As if we would have the chance. Unless it meant Mom was coming home?

Occasionally, Dad took us to the hospital with him, but we had to wait in the car: hospital rules forbade children to visit patients. Dad pointed out Mom's window to us, the second one from the end, on the fourth floor. Once I thought I saw a shadowy figure there, and I waved with both arms. But the sky reflected on the window, and I never really knew if Mom was there or not.

One day, Dad took me downtown with him to the Palliser Hotel.

"Sheila, honey, we're going to meet a very important man," he said, punching the button on the shiny brass panel for the fifth floor. "And I want you to make a good impression on him, so be on your best behaviour."

As the elevator lurched slowly upwards, I spit on the heels of my hands and scrubbed away at the grass stains on my knees. That done, I peered into the bronze panel and tried to smooth out my hair.

Dad rapped at the door of room 504, and after a few minutes, a short, rotund man opened the door. The curve of his grey-suited stomach was at my eye level. A gold chain draped above it, crossing from vest pocket to vest pocket. I raised my eyes to see, above that, piercing blue eyes. There was power there, yet kindness.

"This is my little girl," my father said, hat in hand. "Sheila, this is our province's premier, William Aberhart."

The one on the radio, the one with his *Bible Hour* every Sunday that Mom never missed?

"Yes, sir," Dad was saying to Mr. Aberhart as we stepped inside the room, "it's because of my children that I want this chance to start a tradesmen's union."

"Yes, yes," Mr. Aberhart said abruptly. "I can only spare you a few minutes. Do you have the proposed lien with you?"

Dad handed him a sheaf of papers, and Mr. Aberhart glanced through them quickly before pulling out his watch. "I'm afraid that's all the time I can give you," he said, and he ushered us to the door.

Dad and I found ourselves out in the hallway. "Thank you very much, Mr. Aberhart," said Dad. "I'm sure my daughter Sheila will never forget the day she met the founder of the Social Credit Party."

"My mother's a member of Social Credit," I said loudly to Mr. Aberhart. "She's secretary for the North Hill branch and has been ever since it began. Whenever they had their meeting at our house, I'd play the piano for them. But we had to sell the piano because we had no money left."

Mr. Aberhart's blue eyes lost their coldness. "You didn't tell me this, Mr. Brary," he said, turning to Dad.

"Well, I…"

"My mother's in the hospital now. She's supposed to have an operation because she isn't getting better." I stepped closer to him. "She's been there a long time."

His eyes grew sharper. "I'll look into it," he said, speaking directly to me. I believed him.

Dad started to whistle as soon as we left the hotel to catch the streetcar home. "My, oh my," he said, admiringly. "You can see why the man has got where he is." He paused to look at a man's suit displayed in a store window. "This may be my lucky break," he said, rocking back on his heels. Then we started off again, Dad's steps so brisk that I had trouble keeping up.

Irene left the morning that Mom came home three weeks later. My mother had lost so much weight that her dress hung on her, and her walk was more like a shuffle. The first thing she did was go to the baby. She took one look at him and burst into tears. Loosening his clothing, she checked him all over, even the crack between his buttocks. "Merciful heavens, it's a wonder he's alive," she cried. She turned on my father. "And you paid good money to a housekeeper to look after the children? Look at the cradle cap on this child! Not to mention he's even thinner, if that were possible. If that—that housekeeper of yours—was still here, I'd soon tell her a thing or two about looking after children."

"Now, Agnes, don't get yourself excited," Dad soothed. "You know that's not good for you. Why don't you get unpacked and lie down? I'll attend to everything."

But my mother wouldn't. She took the baby into the kitchen and rubbed olive oil on his scalp. Then she bathed and shampooed him in the kitchen sink.

Dad left minutes later, saying he had business downtown. As soon as his car had driven away, Mrs. Bruce was at the back door, anxious to see Mom.

"You can't know how glad we are to have you home again and on the mend," she said, pressing Mom's hand fervently. "It has been a worrisome time…."

"I know," said Mom. "If it hadn't been for the Social Credit Party—a member came in every day to check I was getting the best of care—I'm sure I wouldn't be here today. They told me that Mr. Aberhart himself got in touch with the specialist Dr. Doyle, and after my surgery, he asked the doctor to put me on that new drug, sulfanilamide."

"Well," Mrs. Bruce seemed to be choosing her words carefully, "I hesitate to tell you this, but…." She caught sight of me and dropped her voice. "Little pitchers have big ears," she said.

"Sheila, run out and play," said Mom quickly. "It's far too nice a day for you to be indoors. And on a Saturday, too."

I did go out but sneaked around the side to listen under the open kitchen window.

"Your husband," I heard Mrs. Bruce say. "He and that woman…. They were trying to get the neighbours to say that you'd been acting crazy even before you went into the hospital. They were trying to convince Dr. Doyle that you should be committed to the insane asylum in Ponoka…."

I heard the scrape of a chair and my mother's sharp cry.

"Oh, yes," Mrs. Bruce went on, "the two of them planned to settle in, real cozy-like. So several of the neighbours—including old Mrs. McLean, and you know she's well over eighty and can barely manage even with a cane—we went to talk to Dr. Doyle ourselves. We let him know what was going on. We told him that you were run off your feet trying to make ends meet, and with no help at all from that no-good man of yours."

I crept away, doubled up with pain.

CHAPTER
eleven

In the days that followed, Mom moved through the house like a shadow. Gone was her usual quick energy and ability to rise before us and work long after we had gone to bed. Instead, she lay down to rest whenever she could, and I often heard her whimpering with pain from the bedroom.

Dad grew impatient with her. "There you are, bawling just like a big calf. The pain is all in your head."

"It's all in my head, all right," said Mom. "My left ear."

"If you paid no attention to it, it would go away."

"Easy for you to say. You're not the one having it."

Her ear drained thick, whitish-green pus that stained the bandage and smelled foul. Mom wanted me to come with her for her weekly visits to the doctor. "I'm too weak to go on my own…. No, not Paul. I already ask him to do too much as it is. The poor boy, he does the best he can to fill in for your worthless father."

The doctor was located downtown in a stone office building with an elevator whose brass fittings gleamed. The odour of the brass cleaner still lingered, and for some reason, I found it reassuring. The elevator man wore white gloves.

The office itself was austere with a brown linoleum floor and three wooden chairs painted chocolate brown. The office even smelled brown, like iodine.

When Dr. Doyle appeared at the door of his treatment room, he asked Mom to step inside. She turned to me. "You come in, too, Sheila," she said. I got to my feet reluctantly.

"Leave the child where she is, Mrs. Brary," the doctor said. "There's no point in her seeing a dressing being changed. She should be in school."

"I want her there with me," Mom said. "It won't hurt her to face the realities of life."

Dr. Doyle bent his head and looked over his glasses at her with sharp eyes, but said nothing.

Inside his treatment room, with Mom seated on a chair before him, he began to slowly pull out what seemed to be yards and yards of stained dressing. My mother started to scream, her legs jittering and her feet tapping out a frantic message of pain, or fear.

Sweat began to run in little rivulets down the back of my knees. The shining silver basin spilled over with blood-stained dressing.

"Tut, tut, now," Dr. Doyle kept saying to Mom. "It's not that bad."

I didn't know what to think. Were all men cruel? Or did she make too much fuss about things? But surely it must be painful.

Mom seemed strangely subdued—almost peaceful—after the visit, and after subsequent visits. It was as if she were relieved, in some way, to vent some of her own awful inner pain.

But I dreaded going with her to the doctor and began to have nightmares the night before each visit. As soon as we stepped into the office building, my heart would begin to flutter, like the piece of cardboard Paul had attached with a clothespin to a spoke in his bicycle wheel.

Mrs. Wadleigh came to visit Mom. "I've brought you a dozen Rhode Island Red eggs. They're fresh from the farm near the slough." She set the basket on the kitchen table. "I want you to make yourself an eggnog every day. The nuns back home taught us a special way. I knew a Sister once who had the same problem as you, and she had an eggnog every day. She was right in no time. You separate the yolk from the white, and beat them separately, then float the beaten white on top of the eggnog and sprinkle with a little nutmeg."

~

Andy had turned from a happy toddler to one who threw tantrums and whined and fussed in-between times. It drove Mom wild.

"Whatever happened to Andy while I was away?" she quizzed me one day. And while I was trying to think of the best way to tell her that he had fallen from his high chair—in spite of Dad's telling me not to—Tom came in with a skinned knee, and Mom's attention turned to him.

Mom always had questions for me about Irene. "Where did this woman sleep?"

"I don't know, Mom. I was always asleep by the time she went to bed."

"There was something going on between your father and her."

"Mom, I don't know!"

"What did she do all the time? She certainly didn't do a lick of housework. The house has never been swept the whole time I was away."

"She sewed."

"Sewed?"

"On her sewing machine. She did alterations for stores."

A look of dawning comprehension came into Mom's eyes, and I realized—too late—my mistake. I had identified Irene as the maker of my costume for the Christmas play.

"So your father has known her for a long time?" Mom persisted.

"I don't know."

"Sheila—"

"Ask Dad!"

Not that Dad was around that much to ask. He was out on the road, first to Edmonton to present a proposed mechanic's lien to the Alberta government, and then—successful at that—to form the Alberta Tradesmen Union. It kept him away most of the time, travelling to all the small towns between Calgary and Edmonton.

"This summer, as soon as school is out, Snooks," he promised me on one of his infrequent visits home, "I'll take you with me on one of my trips."

~

The sun grew warmer each day. Martha and I rolled down our long winter stockings into brown doughnuts around our ankles.

Overnight it seemed, the prairie leapt into growth. Even the ground felt alive, and I flung myself on it to listen, hoping to catch its heartbeat. I heard the *clack* of grasshoppers' legs, the *buzz* of flies, the *whir* of bluebottles. A chorus of birds— cedar waxwings, red cardinals, robins—sang all around me, a dizzy round of praise. By the time I went home, I felt stunned with so much sun and empty space.

I took Andy out to the vacant field directly behind our house and let him build roads for his toy car. We played in an old fire ring—Bill Green had told me once that it was an old fire pit of the Indians—and Andy would zoom his car along its sloping side. I gathered dandelions and made chains, my hands becoming sticky and stained with their milk.

Mom enlisted all of us to help plant most of the backyard in potatoes. Paul dug the holes, and Mom, Tom and I planted the cut potato pieces, making sure each piece had at least one eye. A narrow strip of the garden, near the house, was left for the later planting of carrots, radishes and lettuce.

Mom scrubbed her hands at the kitchen sink afterwards, cleaning the dirt out from under her nails. When she'd dried her hands, she held them up for inspection. "I used to pride myself on my hands; people would often remark on how graceful they were. Now look…. Maybe I was *too* proud," she said pensively.

"I think you have beautiful hands, Mom." I did. I had seen them mend and bake, put bandages on scraped knees, check a child's forehead for fever and turn the pages of a book as she read to us.

Finally, there were no more visits to the doctor, and Mom was feeling better. For the first time in months, I went to sleep without a hard knot in my stomach.

~

On the last day of school, Miss Campbell handed out our report cards and returned our art portfolios. She stopped me on my way out.

"I've enjoyed having you this year, Sheila," she said, smiling at me. "You've done very well in your artwork. I especially liked your last assignment."

I had done that assignment the evening Mom came home from the hospital. I'd been out in the street watching the bigger boys playing Alley, Alley, I-Over and had noticed that bright-green turkey weed had started to blossom between the cracks of the sidewalk outside our house. As I knelt to pick one, a subtle shift in my consciousness made the mountains in the west blaze forth in an incredible purple against a vibrating red sunset. The colours were so iridescent that I couldn't move and remained kneeling until the vision faded, and I was back in the ordinary world. Still in a state of bliss, I'd gone into the house, found my Crayolas and tried to recapture the moment with the yellow-green blossom of the turkey weed, the violet mountains and the crimson sky.

The last day of school was also the last day of Brownies, and the day Brown Owl had promised to announce the winner of the camp holiday in August. I was sure I would win, but a Brownie in another pack on the North Hill had earned one more badge than me. I swallowed hard, trying not to show my disappointment.

CHAPTER
twelve

As promised, Dad took me with him on one of his trips in early July. We stopped at the first gas station on the highway outside of Calgary, a one-pump building badly in need of paint, rusty oil barrels stored along one side.

I wandered over to a field nearby and watched the gophers pop up out of their holes to squeak. Dad signed up the gas station owner with the union and collected the ten-dollar membership fee.

"Ready for a bite to eat?" Dad asked when we were back on the road again. The overhead sun beat down on the roof of the car. The windshield began to become splattered with grasshoppers. "Look over there," said Dad, nodding his head to the west. "Another grain elevator. That means a small town and a Chinese restaurant."

We bumped over the railway tracks and parked on the one street that ran through the centre of the town. Walking past a feed store, a barbershop with its striped red-and white pole outside, and a dry-goods store, we found the Chinese restaurant. Through the dusty windows, we could see three or four people at the counter. "I know these places," Dad said. "Lots of good food and cheap."

Dad chose a booth at one side and sat facing the entrance. I had a view of the kitchen where huge vats on the stove threw off clouds of steam. The surface of the table was dark and greasy and scarred with initials.

"I'll have bacon and eggs," Dad told the elderly Chinese man who appeared silently at our table a few moments later. "And a soft-boiled egg for my little girl…. What kind of pie do you have, Charlie?"

"We got apple, bluebelly, lemon, luhbarb. All out of bluebelly, lemon, luhbarb," the man said.

"Apple pie for me then," said Dad without a blink, "and a strawberry milkshake for my little girl."

The egg, top off, was served in an eggcup with a maroon-and-gold band around the rim and a matching saucer. I took one spoonful of the egg, then set down the spoon.

"What's the matter, honey? Not hungry?"

"It doesn't taste very good," I whispered, not wanting to make a fuss.

Dad reached for the egg and held it up to his nose. "Charlie," he said, calling over the owner, "this Goddamned egg is rotten." I sat motionless. Dad so seldom swore. "No, no, don't bother with another one. Make that a double strawberry milkshake."

Later—back on the highway, the dust from the dirt road clogging my nose and mouth—I begged Dad through clenched teeth, "Stop the car." As soon as I pushed open the door,

I threw up the strawberry milkshake onto the roadside where it trickled down into the dry matted grass.

"Never mind," Dad said to me when I climbed back into the car and took the handkerchief he offered me. "Accidents will happen."

Around three that afternoon, after visiting two more service stations, he wiped his face with his handkerchief and said, "We need to take a break," and pulled over to park on the side of the bank of the Bow River. It was good to be out of the hot car where my legs had been sticking to the leather seat.

The water was warm near the shore, and I walked from sandbar to sandbar, each new pool of water feeling cooler, Finally, I stood knee-deep in the current that flowed with a measured calmness, and I splashed my face and arms, made a cup with my hands and drank until I could drink no more. Gone was the tiredness, heat and dust of the trip. Gone was the memory of the quarrel my mother and father had had before we left Calgary. "Why can't you take me on your trip?" she'd asked. "Don't you think I'd like to get away, too?"

Dad had to clean off the windshields before we set off again. Crusted with dead grasshoppers and running with their tobacco-coloured juice, the windows looked like a battleground. Their corpses clogged air vents and crunched underfoot as I opened the passenger door.

After visiting two more service stations, Dad took a side road that led through a grove of aspens. "A good friend of mine lives around here," he said as we bumped along the ruts, baked by the sun into concrete hardness. We came upon a cottage with shingled walls, set within a garden of hollyhocks and delphiniums, and I caught a glimpse of a river. Dad ran a comb through his hair, straightened his vest and popped a Sen-Sen into his mouth.

Dad's friend was a woman. Not Irene, but like Irene in that she seemed to think Dad belonged to her in some special way. Once more, store-bought cookies and another directive to absent myself for an hour. His watch again.

The river ran cool and clear at the bottom of the land. Two Indian boys played in the river a short distance away, and behind them, several columns of blue smoke rose from a collection of small buildings. I listened to the running water and smelled the pine trees and found myself wishing I could live with the Indians. I stayed away from the cottage until I heard, in the distance, Dad calling my name.

We started back to Calgary. Dad stopped once to stretch and cool off on the bank of the Bow River, running green over sandbars and smooth rocks. I waded into the water, my dress tucked into the elastic of my underpants, and I stayed there until I felt as cool, clean and in a natural rhythm as the flowing river.

~

Dad was home during the week of the Calgary Stampede, and we all took the streetcar to the Stampede. It was a blistering hot July day, the sun striking the Stampede grounds like a bronze gong. The heat, the bright sunlight, the dust from the sawdust kicked up by the crowds and the noise from the rides and hawkers: all of these made Mom feel dizzy.

"Sheila, take your mother to the Red Cross tent," Dad said. "She looks ready to faint."

Inside the tent was dark and cool. A Red Cross nurse—dressed in a grey uniform, with a white apron fastened at the shoulders with straight pins, and a white, fine cotton head-square fastened neatly behind her neck—gave Mom a cup of tea and had her lie down on one of the many cots set up along the sides of the tent. The nurse took Mark, changed his diaper and gave him a bottle of water. Then she sat me at a small table and placed a glass of milk and two graham crackers in front of me. "How old are you?" she asked.

"Almost eight. I'm going into grade three.... I'm going to be a nurse when I grow up." I didn't tell her that this was a decision I had just made.

We found Dad, Paul, Tom and Andy later at the chuckwagon races, cheering on the drivers as their wheels lifted and threatened to overturn the wagons. Mom, pushing the baby buggy, and I went looking for the crafts exhibit. On the way past the livestock building with its rich smells of hay and straw and warm animals, we met Dave Black and his parents coming out.

My mother stopped briefly to chat with Mrs. Black. "I've always wanted to meet you, Mrs. Brary," Mrs. Black said warmly. "I know you are a wonderful mother to have raised a girl like Sheila. You must be proud of your beautiful children."

"Yes," said my mother, "my children are my jewels." I looked at her quickly. I'd never heard her say that before. What she did say was that we were coals of fire heaped on her head.

Later, I asked Dad if I could have a ride on a Shetland pony. I don't know what I was expecting, but I was disappointed at the sight of the dun-coloured creatures whose heads looked too big for their bodies. To be on one was like being on an oversized dog, but one with coarse, scratchy hair.

A man led the pony slowly around the ring. The animal dropped its head down as it plodded dully behind him. It made me think of Mom with her daily plodding through dishes, beds, washing, cooking: her small, dusty circle of duty. With the Shetland pony, there was no sense of spirit, of beauty, none of the soul I'd felt in the horses that had burned in the outbuilding.

"Did you like the ride, honey?" Dad asked.

"Not very. Too slow. I felt sorry for the pony."

"You want to see what I call horses? I'll take you to the Stampede gate where the Indians are camped with their tee-pees and their ponies. Of course, it's all a show for the tourists. You know, Sheila, I respect the Indian far more than I respect any white man. When an Indian gives you his word, he keeps it. They say that the white man talks with a curved tongue, and I've found that to be true."

I wondered who hadn't kept their word with Dad. According to Mom, it was the other way around—it was Dad who didn't keep his word. I found it hard to try to figure them out. They both had their own version of things. It was like the story Dad told about him being the first white baby born in Regina. Dad said that the Indians were curious—they had never seen a white baby—and they kidnapped him. But they returned him to my grandmother two weeks later, saying, "He didn't like our food. He cried too much."

When I asked my mother, she had muttered, "They sent the wrong baby back." Another time she had hinted that Dad's father had had an Indian woman on the side, and that Grandma had to put up with it.

Now Dad was saying to me, "Let's try the merry-go-round."

We walked past booths with tantalizing smells of frying hamburger and onions and over to the gaudily painted rides and their hurdy-gurdy music that moved into my body and took over. I found a small golden-brown horse I liked, and Dad buckled me in with the wide safety strap. He sat on the horse next to me, a black horse with a red mane and protruding brown eyes rimmed with gold. The horses smelt of varnish, and the reins were smooth in my hands. There were bells on the stirrups.

The ride started slowly; the horses moved in long, graceful arcs. But the pace soon picked up, and the music became louder, faster. The horses swept up to dizzying heights, plunged to alarming depths. I wrapped the leather reins tightly around my hand and hung onto my horse's neck.

I looked over at Dad. His head was thrown back, and he was laughing. Then l, too, was caught up in the excitement of the swoop and plummet, the abandonment to the gaudy, almost alive, horses.

When my feet were back on the ground, my head and body still felt as in motion.

"Did you like that ride, honey?"

"Yes!"

I sensed that I was like Dad, the way Mom said, because this was what I wanted from life. Excitement. Not dullness and plodding.

Afterwards, Dad bought all of us hot dogs and candy floss. At the end of the day, catching the streetcar home, we were all so happy and full of the pleasure of the Stampede that we sat—taking up the two front benches—and beamed at each other.

~

Mom phoned city hall about the possibility of summer camp for me. "August would be a good time for you to be out of the city, Sheila, especially since it's the polio season." My mother had two main worries in the summer for us: polio and sleeping sickness. She would never allow us to go swimming more than once a day at the Riley Park pool. "Swimming is very tiring," she said. "Why, look at poor Mrs. McLean's granddaughter. Four years ago, she went swimming one morning, then again in the afternoon, and two days later she came down with infantile paralysis. She'll be a cripple all her life, poor child, and who will take care of her when her parents die?"

A few days after Mom's phone call to the city, a young woman in her late twenties called around to the house just after lunch. "I'm Miss Metcalfe, and I'm from the city," she said when I answered the front door. "Is your mother at home?"

I went to fetch Mom. She was taking the last loaf of bread out of the oven. She took off her apron and went to meet Miss Metcalfe.

"Come in and sit down," Mom said, as she plumped up a cushion on the best chair.

"It's about your daughter, Sheila. We may have a place for her at our Sunshine Camp for Underprivileged Girls at Gull

Lake," said Miss Metcalfe, settling herself and making a quick but thorough survey of our living room.

"Underprivileged?" Mom bridled.

"Now, now, Mrs. Brary," Miss Metcalfe appeased, crossing her legs and swinging her little high-heeled foot so that one pump dropped, exposing her silk-stockinged heel. "The important thing is that Sheila gets a week out of the city, has a chance to swim in the lake and be with other girls. We can give her a little pocket money, too. There's a tuck shop at camp open every day, and the girls all love to buy candy there." She opened her large handbag. "I have a list here of items that the campers are required to bring. Does Sheila have a bathing suit?"

Mom took the offered sheet of paper and placed it face-down on the arm of the chesterfield. "You're all very kind, I'm sure, and just trying to do your job," Mom said in her most dignified voice. But I could tell she was still in a huff by the stiff way she held her shoulders. "Sheila has a perfectly good bathing suit that I knitted for her last summer. As for pocket money, what kind of camp is it that allows children to have candy every day? I certainly don't let my children have it here at home—only once in awhile, as a treat. I'm perfectly sure that candy every day is bad for children, and I am surprised at you for encouraging it."

Miss Metcalfe's foot stopped swinging, and she uncrossed her legs. She leaned forward. "You think about it, and if you should change your mind…. I'm sure there are a dozen girls who would jump at the chance to go away to camp for a week."

"It's not something I do as a rule," said Mom. "Change my mind. Now, if you'll excuse me." Mom stood. "I'm very busy. Sheila, show Miss Metcalfe to the door."

Miss Metcalfe's voice became testy. "If you feel that strongly about it, we'll forego the money allowance for Sheila. We can't have a child miss camp just because...."

"That will be fine," said Mom. "Good afternoon, Miss Metcalfe."

After the social worker left, I picked up the clothes list where Mom had left it on the chesterfield arm. "*Two nightgowns*," I read. Two nightgowns. I didn't even own one nightgown.

I took the list with me into the kitchen where Mom was tipping the loaves of bread out of their pans. "Just listen to all these things they want at camp. Two nightgowns, one toothbrush.... We'd have to buy nightgowns and a toothbrush...."

"We can't afford them. If you go, you can do without. No one's going to be checking up on you. Now instead of always thinking about yourself, go see what Mark is crying about. Maybe his diaper needs changing."

~

The day before I was due to leave for the Sunshine Camp at Gull Lake, Mom called me into her bedroom. She seemed different, remote and cold.

"I have a nightgown for you for camp," she said. "It's in the top dresser drawer."

I opened the drawer and saw, on the top, the orange gown I'd worn in the Christmas play.

"You are to wear this every night at camp. It will remind you of how selfish you are and how you've added to my unhappiness. And here," she continued in the same flat voice and holding out her hand to me. "Here's ten cents for pocket money. Buy yourself some candy."

Could it be that Mom *was* crazy, as Dad said?

thirteen

Miss Metcalfe, the social worker, called on the morning I was to leave for camp to take me to the train station. When I answered the door, she marched in without being invited.

My mother's voice was chilly. "Please have a seat," she said. She seated herself across from Miss Metcalfe. "Sheila's ready. I've packed her a lunch. It's inside her shopping bag with the rest of her things."

Miss Metcalfe's chin went up. "We provide lunch on the train for the girls," she said. "Really, there was no need for you to do that."

Mom flushed and dropped her eyes. She stared at Miss Metcalfe's shoes, alligator this time, with Cuban heels and a wide strap across the instep. Mom slid her own worn house-shoes under her chair, out of sight.

"Sheila has all the required items on the list?" Miss Metcalfe inquired. "Toothbrush, change of underwear?"

"She has what we could manage," Mom answered. "We've no money for nightgowns in this house. She's to wear the costume she insisted on having made for the Christmas play." Her voice deepened in bitterness. "She wanted it badly enough at the time to go behind my back, and I want you to make sure that she wears it every night."

My body flooded with shame.

Later, when Miss Metcalfe and I were seated on the front seat of her Ford coupe, she said, "Your mother's waving from the window." I didn't turn around but gave a half-hearted wave back.

The platform at the train station was crowded with chattering girls lined up for the Sunshine Camp. I didn't know any of them, and no one looked as lonely as I felt. Miss Metcalfe handed me an envelope. "Don't lose this. It's your return train ticket from Red Deer. And here," she added, pressing something hard into the palm of my hand. "I just can't let you go to camp and be the only girl without any spending money."

I looked at the quarter in my hand. "My mother gave me money."

"Oh? How much?"

"A dime."

Miss Metcalfe's upper lip lifted. "So now you have thirty-five cents. You can spend a nickel a day at the tuck shop."

"BOARRDD!!" shouted the conductor, coming along the platform, his square, peaked cap set down right over his ears.

Miss Metcalfe brightened as she beckoned to a tall, harried-looking woman with a few strands of grey in her hair. "There's your leader," Miss Metcalf said to me.

"This is Sheila Brary, Miss Tweedale," Miss Metcalfe said, pushing me forward. "You remember," she said to the woman,

"I was telling you about Sheila?" Her tone of voice, as she said it, somehow made me feel odd and ashamed.

But Miss Tweedale's voice was kind. "Hello, Sheila. Hurry and join the other campers who are boarding. I'll see you once we're underway."

I turned to join the shoving girls but not before I heard Miss Metcalfe say, "Poor thing, I've just given her a quarter for spending money. I told you about her parents. You'd have to meet the mother to believe her. And the father—well!"

"BOARRDD!!"

The train picked up speed outside the city limits, and Miss Metcalfe's words blended into the *clippity-clip* of the train "Poor thing, poor thing," *clippity-clip, clippity-clip.* "Meet the mother," *clippity-clip.* "And the father," *clippity-clip.*

I felt hollowed out, as if I had a big, empty cave inside. I went to the small lavatory at the back of the car and ate one of the sandwiches Mom had packed for me.

Later, sitting by the window and looking out at the fields of ripening wheat that rippled in deep waves beneath the passing wind, I saw Miss Tweedale coming down the aisle. "Everything all right, Sheila?"

"Yes, thank you."

"I think you could do with some company." She turned to speak to the girl across the aisle. "Ivy, this is Sheila's first time away at camp. Come sit with her and tell her all about it."

Ivy was a couple of years older than me: sandy hair, freckles across her nose and cheeks, and narrow, green eyes that seemed to size me up.

"You'll love camp," she said loudly as Miss Tweedale moved down the aisle. Then, dropping her voice, "You've got peanut butter at the corner of your mouth. You're not supposed to eat anything between meals—it's against the rules. Of course, you wouldn't know, being new. This is my third year."

When we got off the train at Red Deer, a school bus was waiting for us. It didn't take long before we were bumping down a dirt road. Glimpses of the lake flickered between the stands of aspen and birch.

The camp itself consisted of several low, unpainted buildings of silver-grey wood. A thin column of smoke rose from one. Trees surrounded the buildings on three sides, and on the fourth lay the lake. It stretched as far as I could see. The sun was hidden behind high, grey clouds, making the lake's surface the same shade of grey. White gulls rode the air currents, like angels might look, I thought. Far out on the lake, white-tipped waves broke and curled.

We followed Miss Tweedale to the dormitory, a huge room with about fifty cots placed close together, within touching distance. I parked my shopping bag at the head of the bed nearest to the door, wondering how I would ever breathe at night with all those bodies around. There were only two windows in the room, one above my bed. I could see the lake from it.

Miss Tweedale raised her voice above the clamour. "As soon as you girls are quiet...will you girls please be quiet? That's better. You have five minutes to put your things away. Then I want you to line up in single file for a tour of the camp. After that, it's quiet time for an hour. Supper is at five."

Supper consisted of two cubes of stewing beef, two pieces of carrot, several hunks of potato, and a sliver of turnip, all stuck fast in a greyish gravy. The stew was followed by a pudding so solid that the dish tipped when I tried to put my spoon into it.

"What is this?" I whispered to Ivy, who was watching me.

"Tapioca, only we call it 'Fish-Eyes-In-Glue.' We always have it first night at camp. If you don't want yours, I'll eat it."

I pushed it across the table to her. "When do we go swimming?" I asked.

"In the morning, at ten."

A sharp whistle sounded from the head table where Miss Tweedale sat with the rest of the leaders. "Too much talking, campers!" said the woman at the head of the table, obviously the one in charge. "I want complete silence for the rest of the meal, or no camp fire."

There was no camp fire after all, because it started to rain after supper, and we ran from the dining hall through the deluge to the recreation hall. There we had a singsong and drank pale, grey cocoa with a thick sludge at the bottom of the cup.

I had been dreading the return to the dormitory, the wearing of the orange costume instead of a nightgown. In desperation, I decided to wear my slip and say that I'd forgotten my nightgown.

The cots were covered with two coarse sheets and a grey blanket. Both the pillow and the mattress were stuffed with straw, and bits of it stuck through the heavy, grey ticking.

My rain-soaked clothing took precious minutes to peel off. I hung my dress and underpants on the nail above my bed and jumped into bed in my slip.

Ivy, two beds away, called out. "You're supposed to wear your nightgown."

"I forgot to bring it," I said, turning on my side away from

"Is there a problem here?" Miss Tweedale, who was supervising, asked.

"It's Sheila," Ivy said loudly. "She's gone to bed in her slip. She says she forgot to bring her nightgown."

"Oh, are you sure, Sheila? Perhaps you just overlooked it. Let's unpack your bag, shall we?" And she began to rummage through my shopping bag.

"What's this?" she asked as she held up the orange costume. "Oh, yes. Now I remember. Miss Metcalfe did mention something about—"

I sat up quickly and snatched it from her hand.

"Well, then," she said vaguely, as if not sure what to do. After a few moments, she hesitantly moved on.

"That's a funny-looking nightgown," Ivy said. She had propped herself up on her elbow and was watching me with bright, inquisitive eyes.

"Why don't you just mind your own damn business," I said under my breath.

"Miss Tweedale! Miss Tweedale!" Ivy called out. "The new girl swore at me!"

"Oh, surely not!" exclaimed Miss Tweedale, hurrying back. "Girls, girls, this is no way to behave. And on the first day of camp, too!"

By this time, I was out of my slip and into the costume. I yanked the covers over my head and stayed like that until the lights were out.

Then I heard sniffles from the younger girls. I heard one call out, tearfully, "Momma, Momma." I felt like bawling myself.

Early in the morning, bursting with the unaccustomed cocoa at bedtime, I made my way to the communal chamber pot that had been placed in the middle of the room. It was an empty oil drum and had a small set of wooden steps leading up to the top of it.

The steps felt wet under my bare feet, and when I perched my bottom over the rim, I found out why. The can was full to overflowing. I added my contribution and paddled back to my bed, sat and dried my feet with the orange costume, put on my clothes, opened the door and went out into the new day.

It wasn't far to the outhouse, and I threw the hated costume down the first hole. Then, feeling as if I'd freed myself of a great burden, I went outside and stayed there, listening to the birds and watching the sky redden. Only when I heard voices and movement from the dormitory did I return. I waited on the porch until the other girls were ready for the washhouse.

Breakfast consisted of half an orange, a bowl of lumpy porridge and a cup of blue milk. Miss Tweedale had listed our "Chores For The Day" on a giant blackboard near the kitchen door, and mine was to clear our table after meals and return the milk jugs to the cooler.

It was on my last trip to the kitchen that I heard a familiar voice call out, "Is that really you, Sheila Brary?"

I turned to see Mrs. Powers, our former boarder, coming in the back screen door with a basket filled with loaves of bread. I looked behind her, half-expecting to see her daughter Grace.

"Well, as I live and breathe," she said, setting down the basket on the scrub table in the middle of the room. She took the milk jugs from my hand. "This is a pleasant surprise. And how is your dear mother? I was so sorry I couldn't come to her when she needed me, but I had double pneumonia."

I told her about the new baby and about Mom being in the hospital. Then I asked about Grace.

"We're both staying with my sister in Red Deer. I come out on the supply truck every morning at six to help out. Though it's hardly home cooking, is it? Not like your mother's. I never met a woman who could make a dollar stretch like your mother, or make a home on next to nothing."

Miss Tweedale came through the swinging kitchen doors. "Sheila, what's keeping you? Is there a problem?"

"I was just talking to—"

"Well, come along, now. We've other chores to do before we go to chapel." I hurried to join her, telling Mrs. Powers that I'd see her later.

As soon as the last dishtowel was rinsed and hung to dry on the overhead wooden rack, we trooped over to the chapel. It was a separate building with an altar built of pale yellow wood. A cross, made of branches, hung above the bible, which was placed mid-centre on the altar. Half the pages of the hymn books were missing, but since we had to sing each verse three times, by the end of each hymn, we knew every word.

After chapel, we changed for swimming. "Is that a home-knit bathing suit?" Ivy wanted to know, her voice rising, as if in disbelief.

I looked down at the brown woollen suit with its band of yellow and orange around the middle. I'd grown since last summer, and the suit stretched too tightly across my stomach. Ivy's bathing suit was made of brightly patterned seersucker. It fit her perfectly, and she was getting bumps on her chest.

"Girls! Girls!" sang out Miss Tweedale. "Really, if you're going to dawdle, we'll have no time left to swim. Follow me!"

The trail to the beach led through scrubby bushes and razor-sharp grass that grew as high as our knees, then we plowed through the coarse, yellow sand to the water. Sheets of jellyfish hung in the warm water like gauzy curtains. My woollen bathing suit started to itch. I swam out, away from the shore, away from the jellyfish, away from Ivy. If only I could swim away from everything. When I tired, I flipped over onto my back and floated. The water was cooler out from shore, and the high, white clouds were like ships' sails, full-blown.

"Sheila!" called out Miss Tweedale's voice. "You're too far out. Come back immediately!"

I swam closer to the shore but stayed away from the group of girls paddling at the shoreline. Floating on my stomach, I opened my eyes and saw grains of sand shifting back and forth with the motions of the tide, making new patterns. I let the waves rock and soothe me.

～

As soon as we filed into the dining hall for lunch, I sensed something was wrong and that it involved me. The adults were staring at me, and when I caught them at it, they glanced away quickly.

Even Mrs. Powers—when I returned the empty milk jugs to the kitchen—seemed changed, concerned.

It wasn't until after lunch, and we were lying on our cots in the dormitory, that I discovered what was going on. It was Ivy who told me.

"Everyone knows all about you now," she said triumphantly. "It's all in the papers."

"What's in all the papers? What papers?"

"It's in the headlines of the *Calgary Herald*. Your father. He stole money."

"You're a liar!" I shouted. I was out the door and heading away from the dorm in spite of Miss Tweedale's protests in the background.

I found a newspaper in the recreation hall. There on the front page was the headline, *"CITY MAN CHARGED WITH FRAUD."* It *was* Dad. The words seemed to leap off the page. *"Obtained money under false pretences and is being tried in criminal court."*

My neck felt as if it had been broken. Crushed, I made my way over to the dining hall, praying that Mrs. Powers would be there.

She was standing at the sink, rinsing carrots. One look at my face and she opened her arms to me. After I'd finished crying, she wiped my face with the corner of her apron, saying, "There, there, now."

"I can't stay here," I said finally. "I'm going home. Mom…."

"Yes, she needs someone with her right now," Mrs. Powers agreed. "She's so…terribly alone with her troubles. You can go in with the supply truck in the morning. Be ready to leave by five, but be sure to talk it over with Miss Tweedale first."

"If you're really sure that you don't want to stay here, Sheila…." Miss Tweedale's voice was anxious. "But I can't help thinking that your mother would rather that you were here and not in the city. After all, this is the Sunshine Camp for girls. To get them out of the hot city. To help them be healthy and strong."

"No," I said.

"I'll get you up at five, then," she said, unwillingly. "I'm sorry I can't go with you to see you off, but I'm needed here. Will someone be meeting you in Calgary?"

"I know how to take the streetcar," I said quickly, thinking of the many times I'd gone downtown with Mom to see Dr. Doyle. "I can get home by myself."

As I waited for the train, I saw a patch of turkey weed growing alongside the track. It was sprinkled with fine ash from the train, but in spite of the dusting, the golden buds gleamed and the ferny leaves glowed. The sight of its sturdiness, as always, lifted my heart.

The house was quiet within. Even though I'd been away, my feet remembered the slant of the living-room floor, and the sight of the shabby furniture was reassuring. Through the kitchen window, I saw Tom and Andy in the back yard.

I tiptoed to Mom's bedroom where she always lay down for a nap in the afternoon. "Is that our Sheila?" her voice asked drowsily. I stepped inside. Mark was asleep beside her with only a light sheet covering him. The blind had been pulled down so that it was dark and cool in the bedroom, in contrast to the blazing hot afternoon I had just come through.

Mom's eyes flew open. "Why are you here and not at camp?" she asked, surprise lifting her voice.

"I didn't like it. The food was no good. The milk was blue. We could only go in swimming when they said."

"So home is not so bad, then, after all?"

"No."

Mom's hand crept over to touch mine. "I'm glad you're home. I know I'm often terribly cross with you, Sheila, and it must seem that I'm harder on you than on the boys. But I want you to be strong and good. It's not easy to be a woman, God knows, but the world needs good, strong women."

CHAPTER
fourteen

Dad and Mom never spoke directly to us about the trial. I overheard their late-night conversations from the kitchen as I lay, half-asleep, on the chesterfield.

"I went to the lawyer today," said Dad, "but before we were fifteen minutes into the conversation, he said he wanted a retainer before he would handle the case. When I told him I had no money, his answer was to show me to the door."

Mom's voice was tentative. "You could sell the car."

"No," Dad said firmly. "I need it for my job. We'll just have to use this month's mortgage payment if I'm to have any representation at all. A friend of mine was telling me about a lawyer who has handled these kind of cases before and never lost."

"We're already two mortgage payments behind as it is," Mom said faintly.

"It will have to be three."

"But to take the chance of losing the house after all these years…."

"I've tried borrowing, Agnes. Everyone is in the same boat, and there's no money to be had. We have no choice."

Mom sighed, and I heard the drum of her fingers on the enamelled table top. "Frank," she said at last, "if there was a chance that you could learn from this…learn to leave the women alone…be true to your own family…."

"Give me that chance, Agnes," he begged. "You'll never regret it. You know that you and the kiddies mean the world to me."

I lay rigid, waiting to hear Mom's answer. I'd heard Dad make these same promises before and break them. Why should this time be any different?

"You must give me your word, before God as your witness, Frank Brary."

"You have it. I swear it on my mother's head."

I wanted to shout, "Liar! Liar!" And then—somehow—I felt guilty. He was my father, and I was supposed to honour him. It was one of the Ten Commandments we'd learned at Sunday School. And if my mother could be loyal to him after all he'd done, maybe I was supposed to be loyal, too. Maybe this is what Mom meant when she'd said she wanted me to be a strong and good woman.

~

The city shimmered under the hot August sun. Far on the western horizon, the pale blue shapes of the mountains seemed to float above the foothills. Mom uncoiled a new flypaper and attached it with a thumbtack to the kitchen ceiling. Within moments, two flies had landed on its sticky surface, and they buzzed and struggled in the heat to free themselves.

I called on Martha to go swimming at the pool in Riley Park. "I'm sorry," Martha's grandmother said when she answered the door. "Martha had a bad night last night with her asthma, and she's sleeping right now."

So I went by myself and spent the whole afternoon learning to do the back crawl.

~

Dad took me downtown with him to see his new lawyer. "William George Dawson" was the name painted in black letters on the frosted glass panel. Inside, it smelled of cigars. A secretary, seated behind a huge black typewriter, seemed to know Dad, and I saw—with a familiar lurch in my stomach—how her eyes widened as she smiled at him. He leaned forward slightly, his own eyes brighter, their grey becoming almost blue.

Mr. Dawson, prosperous and shrewd looking, greeted Dad as if they were old friends and in this mess together. I sat on one of the hard oak chairs and watched them shake hands and clap each other on the shoulder. They were alike, I thought, as I listened to them plot their strategy. I didn't trust either of them. I scratched away at an old mosquito bite on my ankle until it bled into my sock.

~

People in the neighbourhood began to look the other way whenever we met on the street. Mom was so worried about how to get enough money for the lawyer that the neighbours' attitude was far down on her list of things to be concerned about.

Things changed for me at school. My grade three teacher wasn't as friendly to me as Miss Campbell had been, and my classmates treated me differently, too. I thought it must be because of my father's troubles.

My mother kept all the newspaper clippings, from the first headline with its charge against Dad to the final headline, which didn't come until February: *"INSUFFICIENT EVIDENCE TO CONVICT CITY MAN."*

"Merciful God in heaven," Mom exclaimed. "With all the news coming out of Europe, and the talk of war, have they nothing better to do than blazon this across the front page?"

After a while, some of the neighbours began to say hello again. Mom was slow to warm up. "As if all of us don't have something to be ashamed of, if the truth be known," she said with a toss of her head.

Even though the trial was over, Mom seemed strung tight, and she threw herself into a frenzy of baking and cooking. We had jelly roll; we had johnnycake swimming in corn syrup; we had doughnuts with special coatings of ground-up peanuts, coconut or icing sugar. Pans of toffee, fudge and peanut brittle appeared. Root beer brewed in the basement, a lovely, licorice smell wafting up the cellar stairs.

I wondered, briefly, where the money had come from. Meat appeared less often on the table, so I thought that Mom might have shifted the money around. Sweets were what she craved, and sweets were what we got.

The news from Europe alarmed everyone in our neighbourhood. In mid-March, the Germans took over Czechoslovakia, and people predicted that Poland would be next.

"Britain will declare war on Germany, and it will be our young men who will be sent to the front," they said. "The

English will be the officers, and our boys the cannon fodder. It's 1914 all over again."

Mom looked at Paul, a shadow in her eyes. "Pray God that if there is a war, it will be over before Paul is of age." She wasn't as concerned about Dad. "They would never take you, Frank," she said. "At fifty-four, you're past enlistment age."

Dad shot Mom a hostile glance. "Don't be so quick to say that. They'll be mighty glad to get an able-bodied man who has all his tickets in machinery from steam right through to diesel."

~

The grass in the empty field behind our house and on the foothills started to turn green. The previous October, the neighbourhood men had burned off the prairie wool on all the empty land around. Standing with wet gunny sacks, ready to beat out the fire if it threatened to spread towards the foothills, they had surveyed the charred fields with satisfaction. With grimy face, and clothes pungent with smoke, one of the men had spat and said, "That ought to do her. The grass will be greener, come next May, in time for the King and Queen's visit."

The royal visit would be the first time a reigning monarch had visited Canada, and everyone was making plans. Mr. Bruce already had a Union Jack flying from his front porch. The neighbourhood women had been up and down our street, removing any paper or debris that the winter had left buried beneath the snow.

The Brownies were to line up on 16th Avenue, part of the route to be taken by their Royal Highnesses. Mom grumbled as she sprinkled my Brownie uniform with warm water and plugged in the iron. "Sure, aren't they coming over here just to get us to side with them if England goes to war?" She tested the iron with a finger moistened on her tongue. "I wouldn't go across the street to see them, myself. Not that I'm saying anything personal against them. King George is a far better man than his brother, the Duke of Windsor. Imagine taking up with a married woman!" She gave the uniform a heavy thump with the iron. "The Queen is a nice enough woman and a good mother. *And* she's not English, which is all to the good." The iron weaved back and forth. "What the English kings and queens have done to Ireland is beyond belief...."

"That's all ancient history, Mom," Paul said, who was polishing his boots. "You're living in Canada now."

Mom was indignant. "Ancient history, is it? Well, it's not that long ago that Oliver Cromwell...and the same atrocities are going on in Ireland right now!"

"In our history book it says—"

"Your history books are all wrong. They were written by the English, so what else do you expect? You don't for one minute think you're getting the truth of it, do you?"

~

The King and Queen arrived in Calgary at the end of May. The sky was an incredible blue, vaulting high over the prairies, which were a lush green. All along both sides of 16th Avenue, wild flowers shone in the sunshine: buffalo beans, black-eyed Susans, sweet peas and pink single-petal roses with a fragrance as delicate as their colour.

The Queen wore a blue dress, a matching blue duster and an off-the-face hat of the same shade. She nodded and smiled, first to one side, then to the other. A sigh of pleasure went through the crowd, followed by a spatter of applause. Her small white-gloved hand waved graciously. The King, dressed in a naval uniform, looked ill at ease and shy but determined and much taller and more handsome than in his photographs.

The cavalcade passed slowly, but it was all over in a few minutes. Nevertheless, for the rest of the day we were caught up in the bubble of excitement of the royal visit. Canadian and British flags snapped and flung their colours in the wind, and the sound of brass bands was heard all over the city until we went to bed that night.

A registered letter came addressed to Mom. It was notice of foreclosure on our house by the bank because of missed mortgage payments.

Mom sank onto the nearest chair, dropping the letter to the floor as if contaminated. "I'll go to the bank manager tomorrow," she declared when she regained her composure. "Surely, when I tell him our troubles…. I'll ask our landlord Mr. Pickard to tell the bank manager that I'll pay whatever I can, whenever I have even ten dollars…." Her voice petered out, and a keening sound came from deep within her. Then, "No, I don't suppose a bank manager would be too sympa-thetic with our involvement with the law."

She went to see the bank manager, anyway. I watched her hat, with its bright bird wing along one side, go up the street as she made her way to catch the streetcar.

I saw her when she returned. Pity stabbed my heart at the sight of her slumped shoulders and the look of dejection on her face. She looked fifty, instead of thirty-nine.

Mom was quiet the rest of the day. After the younger boys had gone to bed for the night, she arranged pen and paper on the kitchen table. "I'll write to Mrs. Powers," she said. "She might find it in her heart to lend me the money, enough so that we don't lose the house. For fourteen years now, I've managed to keep ahead of the payments. Twenty dollars some months. Other months, thirty, and another ten before the month was up. Surely—if they see I can pay one month's payment—they'll give me time to make up the missing months."

Mrs. Powers must have replied by return mail, and in the envelope was a cheque for the exact amount that Mom had asked for. But when Mom and I took it downtown to the bank manager's office, he said it was too late. "Everything has been set in motion, my dear Mrs. Brary. After all, business is business. Much as I might like to help you personally…. You do understand?"

My mother returned Mrs. Powers cheque. "How good of her it was to send it! She probably asked her people to lend it to her." Mom sighed. Then she straightened her shoulders. "Well, all I can say is bad cess to the bank and to all those who grind down the poor."

There followed days of a frantic search for a house to rent, but no one wanted five children. Each classified section was gone over thoroughly, including those in *The Family Herald* and *The Winnipeg Free Press Prairie Farmer* that Mrs. Wadleigh—originally from Manitoba and still subscribing to both newspapers—passed on to us.

"The good Lord will provide for us in his mercy," breathed Mom in prayer. "He led his chosen people out of the wilderness, and he will do the same for us." But I noticed that her face was gaunt with strain and her eyes shadowed, and I wasn't at all sure God would come through for us.

Every lead my mother followed came to a dead end. Until the day she came upon an ad in *The Calgary Herald*:

Small dairy farm with house in coastal community
20 miles from Vancouver, looking for a man and
wife to operate same. Contact J.D. Chalmers, Box 55,
Calgary Herald.

For the first time in weeks, my mother's voice sounded hopeful. "This sounds just right for us," she said to Dad. "We've both grown up on farms, and you know machinery—they'll be glad to get us." She circled the ad and handed the newspaper to him. "It will be good for the children, too," she added. "And for you. No more cold winters. How many times have you had pneumonia now? Five? The last time I thought I'd never nurse you through it." Her eyes lit up. "Think of it. The ocean…the mountains…this is surely the answer to our prayers."

And so it was arranged. Two special rate Vacation Coach tickets were purchased for the end of June on the CPR to Vancouver; children travelled free. We had tried to locate the coastal community on the map but were unable to find it. "It must be too small," Dad said, and his mouth turned down petulantly.

"We're allowed just so much baggage on our tickets, and that's all," Mom told us children. "That means one cardboard box each for your things." One medium-sized cardboard box was not much. Once I had packed my clothes in it, there was little room for anything else. I gave all my treasures—except my artwork—to Martha: cutout dolls, skipping rope, jacks and ball.

Besides the money from her equity in the house, Mom hoped to make a few dollars from the sale of our furniture. "If I could get fifty dollars," she told me, "it would tide us over until we get settled. Mr. Chalmers wrote that there will be no wage, although we get the house rent-free. Any milk that we can sell, we can keep that money. But the tourist season is almost over, and apparently there are only three cows at present, only one milking."

A second-hand man came and looked with disdain at the worn chesterfield in the living room, the dressers in the bedroom whose drawers stuck and whose varnished tops had become stained and ringed over the years. "This stuff's not worth carrying away," the man said. "I should charge you for taking it off your hands."

My mother was quick to lose her temper, and I watched the faint pink of blood start in her throat and work up to her face. She made a visible effort to control herself. "I couldn't let you have the furniture until next week, anyway," she said, her voice trembling. "Let me think about it."

"No, I don't want to make a second trip," complained the man. "I'll give you forty dollars for the lot, take it or leave it."

While Mom spluttered with indignation, I spoke up. "Make it sixty," I said, "and you can take it right now."

The man gave a surprised bark of laughter. "Done," he said, "but it's more than it's worth. Lucky for you, lady, that you've got yourself a smart girl there."

"Too smart for her own good," Mom said with a sideways glance at me.

"She'll go a long way in this world."

"All right, sixty dollars," said Mom. "We'll have to sleep on the floor and eat off our laps, but…."

The man counted out the money from a worn wallet, and my mother, after recounting, put the money away carefully in her purse. Later, while he loaded our furniture into his truck parked in the back lane, my mother said to me, "Sheila, that was very bold of you to speak up in that way."

But I didn't care. She had the money she wanted, and I had been told I was a smart girl who was going to go a long way.

~

Our last morning in Calgary, Mom went into the back yard and looked all around, as if to imprint in her mind the only home she'd ever owned, although it had never been paid off. The house she'd lost. My heart hurt to see her.

I felt Dad come up behind me where I watched at the pantry window. "Well, I hope your mother's satisfied," he said, anger in his voice. "I'm certainly not in favour of leaving Calgary." He paused for a few moments. Then, "I know what she's up to," he said softly. "She wants to get me away from my friends. Well," and his voice hardened with obstinacy, "she'll see how far this will get her."

fifteen

We spent the night on the train, napping as best we could in the upright seats. Mom had us take turns stretching out on two seats while the rest of us walked up and down the aisle, or from car to car. By the time the train arrived in Vancouver the next morning, we were all hot and tired and grumpy. Mark had developed a rash on his face, and Mom was taking Aspirins, something she did only as a last resort. Dad had spent most of the previous evening in the Club Car, and his eyes were bloodshot.

Dad found a room for us in the St. Francis Hotel on Hastings Street opposite the CPR train station. The manager put in two extra folding cots. "No running in the hallways, you kids," he said. "Or you'll be out on the street." That night, Paul, Tom and Andy slept in the double bed, I slept across the foot. Mom and Dad each took one of the cots, and Mom took Mark in beside her. But he was so restless, she finally put him on a folded blanket on the floor beside her cot.

Outside our hotel window, streetcars clanged, boats whistled and ambulances wailed. Dawn was edging a border of light along the sides of the blinds when a fight broke out in the street below. There were loud shouts of profanity and the smash of bottles on the pavement.

I slid out of bed to peek out from behind the blind. The drunks were already staggering down the street in opposite directions. Opening the window, I leaned out to see the morning. The air was tangy with salt from the ocean. Smells of tar, oil and roasting coffee drifted up from the wharves below Hastings Street. I could smell hot, burnt cinders from the trains across the street. A seagull flew down and perched at the end of the window ledge.

The rest of the family began to get up slowly. Mom put out oranges, bread and butter—she'd bought them the night before—on the top of the dresser. Dad walked across the street to the train station to arrange to have our baggage taken to the Union Steamship dock, and I went with him. While he was busy with the clerk, I stepped outside and hung over the railing of the CPR dock nearby to gawk at the *Empress of Japan* berthed below. A fresh breeze came across Burrard Inlet from the green, forested slopes of the North Shore beyond. I breathed deeply, entranced with this new, beautiful world.

~

The Union Steamship's *Lady Pam* was a graceful, one-funnelled ship with a bow like a clipper ship. She called in at every small settlement along the coast, announcing her arrival with a blast of her steam whistle: one long, two short, and one long. The sound echoed back from the mountains that rose on each side of the narrow, deep channels.

Paul, Tom and I climbed straight, steep steps to the upper deck and leaned on the railing. The water below us was jade green. We sailed past rocky points where seals sunned themselves. A billowing cloud of steam hung over the end of one of the channels, and a tug pulling a long boom of logs headed that way.

"Paul, is the tug going to a pulp mill up there?" asked Tom, pointing to the cloud of steam.

Paul didn't bother to answer but moved down the railing away from us. He had been strangely quiet most of the trip.

After a moment, I joined him. "What's the matter, Paul?" I asked.

"I get so fed up with this whole family," Paul said finally. "I think it's crazy. Mom and Dad do what they want, and it… isn't fair."

I knew that Paul was unhappy about Mom turning to him so often for help. "I won't be a nuisance to you anymore, Paul, I promise," I said.

"It's not you." His face darkened. "Why did we have to move? It wasn't so bad as long as I had my friends. I blame Mom."

He left me then, and I didn't see him again until we reached our destination at noon.

We were all surprised to see only a few cottages strung out on both sides of the government wharf, several with rowboats pulled up on the shore before them. We searched for any sight of a dairy barn but saw nothing but green forest.

There was a store and combined post office at the head of the wharf. The proprietor, a short, bustling man with white bushy eyebrows who said his name was Mr. Norman, directed us to a trail about fifty feet from the store that led into the forest. "It's a fair piece to walk," he said. "Especially with the little ones. Give me a minute to find someone to mind the store, and I'll give you a lift over in my truck. You children wouldn't mind riding in the back of a truck, would you?"

We scrambled up on the flat back to sit among coils of rope, empty wooden boxes and a pile of gunnysacks. Mom, with Mark on her lap, and Dad were squeezed into the cab with Mr. Norman. The truck strained up the steep hill from the wharf to the highway, turned right, clattered over a wooden bridge and finally stopped with a jerk in front of a one-level, unpainted house. Its new wood glistened white under the July sun.

Once inside, we found that there was running water, but no electricity. The bungalow had two bedrooms and a roughed-in bathroom without fixtures. An outhouse was set in a clump of alders at the end of a little path and beyond loomed a mountain. I could hear the chatter of the creek running nearby.

Tom and I set off exploring. We found the barn—much larger than the house—painted crimson with double doors. Inside were stalls for a dozen cows, with a hayloft above. Three Jersey cows stopped chewing their cuds long enough to stare at us. Names were painted in black letters on their stalls: Honey, Silver and Blackie.

While Mom and Dad talked to Mr. Chalmers, Tom and I raced to the beach for a swim. All along the water's edge were tiny, pink shells no bigger than a fingernail, and they were strung along the shoreline like a long necklace. The salt water was surprisingly cold, but buoyant, and when at last I threw myself on the hot, white sand, I felt that we had arrived in paradise.

Every day found new excitements—for everyone, that is, but Paul and Dad who both remained glum. As for Dad, no sooner had we got settled than he was off.

"I'm going to Gibsons," he announced one morning at breakfast, naming the small town about three miles up the coast. He pushed his teacup across the table to be refilled. "I hear there's a garage there, and they may need a good mechanic."

My mother made a lunch for him in tight-lipped silence.

It was late when Dad got home that night. We had all gone to bed, except for Mom, who sat mending by the light of a candle. Once again, I was sleeping in the living room—Tom had confiscated the roughed-in bathroom as his bedroom—so I heard everything.

"A fine time to be traipsing in," Mom complained. "I suppose you've made a lot of new friends, as per usual, and you completely forgot you had a little family waiting for you."

"Don't start in on me the minute I get in the door," Dad said wearily.

"Start in on you, is it? What else would you expect? It's nearly midnight!" And on and on they went until finally I shut out their quarrel by putting the pillow over my head.

In the morning, they took up where they had left off. "Now Agnes," said Dad in a patient voice, "we have to face facts. There's very little work to be had here along the coast. It's as bad as Calgary. Except these people do have fish in the ocean and fruit on the trees, plus all the wood they need to keep themselves warm in the winter, so with mild winters, they're not going to freeze. But work...there's no work to be had. I spoke to a dozen people yesterday—that's why I was home late last night—and they all have the same story. No, if I want work, I'll have to go into Vancouver to find it."

"But Frank...."

"Don't you worry about it for one minute. Paul is old enough to help with the milking, and the other kiddies can pitch in, too. There's no earthly reason for you...."

Mom slammed the kettle on the stove. "So we're right back where we started from. You go off and do what you want, and I'm left at home with the children and no money. Only now I have to cope with running a dairy farm, stoking a wood fire and washing on a scrub-board. I curse the day I met you, Frank Brary."

Dad left for Vancouver the following day. We didn't hear from him until two weeks later, a single-page letter with an enclosed twenty-dollar bill.

I've found a job with Vivien's Machine Shop here in Vancouver, and I like it mighty fine. I'll bring a battery radio up with me the next time I come. Love to you and the kiddies.

Dad

Mom tucked the money away carefully in her purse and put the letter behind the kitchen clock. Her face had softened, and she made us a jellyroll for dessert.

But I heard her crying that night. In the morning, I asked her why.

"Sure, it's all the heavy work I'm doing," she said, moving stiffly around the kitchen. "My muscles are so sore, they wake me during the night. The women here in Canada work harder than we ever did back home in Ireland. All I can say is that I'm doing a hired man out of a job. I saw it first on the Prairies when I came to Canada in 1921. The way those women worked on the homesteads in northern Saskatchewan, it was a corker. No wonder they looked upon themselves as equal with the men! Well, at least I have all the running water I need here in BC."

Over the weeks, Mom grew stronger and was able to sleep throughout the night. And she was sick less often than she had been in Calgary.

She and Paul rose at six every morning to milk the cows. Paul hated milking the cows. "I wished we'd never moved from Calgary," he complained to Mom. But her face was always more peaceful after she'd been with the animals. It was as if she'd returned to a quieter, gentler rhythm within herself.

We sold only a few quarts of milk and a few pounds of butter to Mr. Norman at the store. Most of the summer visitors were wary. "It's because the milk isn't pasteurized," Mr. Norman explained to Mom.

"Sure, haven't the cows been tested for TB every year?" Mom argued. She turned to two customers who happened to be in the store at that moment. "You can come and see for yourselves," she stated. "The certificates are nailed right there on the barn wall."

Mom turned back to Mr. Norman who was looking embarrassed. "I don't believe that heating milk to such a high temperature can be good for it. It stands to reason it must kill some of the goodness in it. I want you to know that I wash each animal's milk bag and udders before I milk her. The cream separator is scalded after each use. I scrub the floor of the milk house with a stiff brush and hot, soapy water every day. The milk is kept icy-cold with the water piped from the creek. Look at my children! Do they seem to be suffering from TB?"

The customers paid for their purchases quickly and left.

We did drink a lot of the rich Jersey milk. For the first time I could ever remember, we were allowed, even encouraged, to drink as much as we wanted. Paul sometimes drank two quarts a day. He was growing quickly, Mom said. She urged us to slather butter thickly on our bread. We had cream on our porridge every morning. We had milk puddings and creamed soups, and milk was used in the baking of bread instead of the usual water.

We had never eaten so well. A Norwegian neighbour woman who lived across the creek brought over eggs from her Leghorns, vegetables from her garden and a sample of whatever she was baking that day. Blackberries began to ripen under the hot August sun. The boys caught salmon nearly every day. Our family fattened.

Then Dad wrote that he would be home at the end of August. Added to that excitement was the fact that school would be starting soon. Mr. Norman had told us that the school bus stopped at the road up from the government wharf. "You children will be the only ones taking the bus from here," he said. "Now, I've got to warn you. People around here are slow to warm up to strangers. It takes them about twenty years to figure that you're going to stay."

We expected Dad home on the noon boat, and we had all made special preparations. Mom baked two blackberry pies.

Paul shovelled out the barn and hosed it down. Tom filled the wood box to overflowing with cedar kindling and split alder. Andy had on his new red socks in honour of Dad's homecoming.

I had made a small rock garden on both sides of the front steps, choosing the whitest and most symmetrical stones I could find in the creek bed and toting them home in the wheelbarrow. I'd found thick green moss growing on a fallen cedar log in the woods and placed it between the stones. That very morning I had finished off by edging the path with fluted clamshells. "Come look, Mom," I'd said, dragging her out to look at it.

"It is very nice, Sheila," she said. "You have artistic talent for sure."

Out of the corner of my eyes, I caught a glimpse of red, then another. Both Mom and I turned to see Andy running up and down the dips of the path to the barn, his red socks flashing like flags in the bright morning sunlight.

"It's strange," said Mom with a look of tenderness on her face, "how the twinkle of Andy's red socks in the sun gives so much pleasure. Such a simple little thing."

I bent to pick up a yellow alder leaf on the path, then flung it from me abruptly. It was a slug, something we hadn't had in Calgary.

I was the only one to go meet Dad at the boat. He seemed different, preoccupied, I thought. But when he hugged me, he smelled the same: cigarettes and Sen-Sen and after-shave lotion.

Mom was waiting outside the front door. She had a shy smile on her face. Mom and Dad didn't embrace, but then they never did, at least not in front of us children.

Mr. Norman arrived in his truck about ten minutes later. He brought along the radio and its B battery that Dad had sent up as freight on the *Lady Pam*. He and Dad set it up in the living room.

Later that afternoon, I went outside with a pail of water for the moss in my rock garden. As I rounded the corner of the house, I saw Dad standing still. He seemed to be looking down at my garden. Then I noticed a stream of yellow liquid splashing against the white stones. A smell like tomcat came wafting over to me. It took a moment for me to realize what Dad was doing. I edged backwards until I was out of sight and then bolted for the trail that led towards the mountain.

I stayed away all afternoon. Taking a different way back home, I came upon a gathering of abandoned shacks. Mr. Norman had told us that a group of deserters from the First World War had hidden somewhere up in the mountains. There was an old apple orchard with branches grey with lichen but that still bore fruit—hard, wizened little green knobs.

Between the gnarled trees and as far as I could see was a spread of turkey weed. I sank to my knees, their foliage springy beneath me, and the scent of pineapple rose up from the hard little blossoms. Always when I seemed to need it most, turkey weed was there.

~

We never missed the news on the radio. On the Sunday of Labour Day weekend, the announcer's voice cracked with tension. "Today, Great Britain declared war on Nazi Germany, and the Canadian government is expected to follow with its own declaration shortly."

Dad got up from his chair and began to pace up and down the kitchen. "I'm going into the city on the next boat and join up. The air force will be glad to get an experienced mechanic like me."

I glanced at Mom. Apprehension, then sorrow, crossed her face.

Dad left the next day on the Union boat. "It has to be," was all my mother said. I went down to the wharf to see him off. My brothers had said their good-byes at home awkwardly. Mom had walked with Dad only as far as the road, then had turned and gone back to the house.

Dad was in a hurry to get away. He walked so fast I had trouble keeping up to him, and once he was up the gangplank, he disappeared down the stairs that led to the dining salon. He never looked back. I stood on the wharf and watched the ship until it disappeared around the Point and out into the open water of the Strait of Georgia.

I wandered home. It was the end of something that I couldn't even put my mind around. Stopping at the moss garden I had made—it seemed like such a long time ago—I kicked at the moss until it was in shreds. Then I piled the stones in two heaps, one on either side of the front door.

⌒

Tom and I were in the same classroom at our new school at Gibsons, even though he was in grade three and I was in grade four. Our teacher was a large, freckled woman who had an invalid husband, and he was worked into our lessons.

"Now, my dear husband has been ill for years, and during the Depression, I was hard-pressed to serve him food that he could digest, was healthful and yet within our limited income. What did I do? At the close of each day, I went to the grocery store and bought up all their over-ripe bananas. Ten cents, and I had enough to feed him for a whole day. Yes. Bananas! Never forget that, class. Bananas are a cheap and wholesome food."

Several weeks later, Dad wrote that he had been accepted into the air force. "He's lied about his age to get in," Mom said, but I could see that she felt proud of him.

Paul was elated. "I'm going to join the air force, too, when I'm old enough. I'm going to be a pilot." Paul was already in cadets at school.

An allotment cheque from the government came soon after that. Mom sank down into the kitchen chair when she saw the amount of the cheque, and the hand holding the cheque trembled. "So much," she whispered, "one hundred and twelve dollars. The government's given me a wife's allowance and one for each of you children. Not only that, but the same amount will be coming in every month and straight to me." Her eyes became brilliant. "I'll even be able to put some money aside each month. Just think. In time, I might be able to buy some land of our own."

Epilogue

~

All of this happened a long time ago. My mother did buy land, and my brothers built a house on it for her. And, for the first time, she had money of her own, money that came in the mail every month, money she could count on. With the money, she had power and with that came self-confidence.

Dad seldom spent his yearly leave from the air force with us, and at the end of the war, Mom told him not to bother coming home again. He never did, though Paul and I saw him a few times over the years. He had married again. His new wife phoned me once and asked about the value of the property Dad had told her he owned on the Sunshine Coast. "He doesn't own any," I said. "It's in my mother's name." She didn't believe me. I said, "Haven't you learned yet that my father lies?"

Paul still doted on Dad and blamed Mom. It was the reverse for me. Dad wanted to be friends with me, accused me of being cold, but I told him I owed my loyalty to Mom. "She was there when we needed her." Paul was with Dad when he died a few days after having a heart attack. I was living in

California at the time and didn't bother coming back for the funeral.

My mother and our neighbours helped to build St. Mary's Catholic Church at Gibsons. After Tom had given her a correspondence course in English 100 for a Christmas present, she began to write and publish award-winning short stories. She died at ninety, but she did not have what every good Catholic prays for, a good death. Painful memories from all her years past came back in an alarming deluge of dread and panic.

I seldom dream about her. I wish I did because in her last years, I grew to appreciate and love her more. I miss her.

But I've been dreaming about horses again, great dark-eyed horses with sleek coats, hot and moist, under my hands and whose breath is as alive as yeast. The dreams make me feel like a child again, with a child's acute senses and perceptive vision.

I've written down how I saw things as a child. But I was left with what bothers me the most, the horror of her last days and the fact that I wasn't with her when she died in the hospital at one o'clock in the morning. I had wanted to be there with her, to let her know I loved her.

I had hoped that her religion would give her peace at the end. It did not seem to. She had hallucinations—a small black dog that repeatedly tried to attack her—and she would scream out in terror. I could never calm her. Other times she cried in the night—like a lost three-year-old—for the great-aunt who had raised her. "Eliza! Eliza!"

The patient in the next bed, an elderly woman who had once been our neighbour, would get out of bed and calm her.

"Hush, hush, child. I'm here." She would stay holding Mom's hand until she slipped back into sleep.

The doctors did everything they could. Early on in her hospitalization, they had a psychiatrist see her—they weren't sure if the hallucinations were from the medications she was taking, or if she had (and had always had) a mental illness.

After examining Mom thoroughly, the psychiatrist, a tall, thin man with a face devoid of any emotion, called me into his office. "From what you've told me," he began as he looked at a space over my left shoulder, "your mother was born at the beginning of the century and within twelve months of her life had turned from a healthy baby into an ailing child, apparently from a smallpox vaccine-induced meningitis. She developed infections in both her eyes and ears, and lost the sight in the left eye and the hearing in the right ear. On several occasions, she was sent away from her large family in Belfast for years to be taken care of by her spinster great-aunt Eliza in the country. Add to that, the First World War, her immigration to Canada and her common-law marriage to a scoundrel. That was a scandalous thing to do in the 'twenties and caused her to be ex-communicated from the Catholic Church. Then there was the Depression of the 'thirties and another World War…. You say that your mother was angry and bitter most of the time when you were growing up. It is small wonder. She had every right to be."

For the first time, he looked at me directly, "The question is not, 'Is she—or has she ever been—mentally ill?' but, 'How did she manage to do as well as she did?' To have raised a family single-handedly—and you tell me you and your brothers are all professionals with families of your own—and then to have lived independently until she was ninety. Still chopping her own kindling, you say. I would say that she showed exemplary courage."

~

The horses. Last night I dreamt that God had caused the Red Sea to close over the Egyptian horses and drown them. And I recoiled in terror, with the same anguish I had felt when I saw my mother stricken with a number of small strokes that led up to the major one causing her death. The sounds of the drowning horses were the screams of my mother. I found the sound of the horses' screams intolerable. I went down to the horses, to comfort and be with them as they died.

The horses. Oh, the horses! Just when I thought I could bear it no longer, I saw a look of peace steal into their eyes. And I knew—then—that God was there with them, even before me. As He must have been with my mother.

Mary Razzell

~

When Mary's three children were in high school, she took a night school writing course, and shortly afterward sold an article she had written for the class. That was her first successful foray into the world of writing, and since then she has had a number of stories, poetry and articles published as well as eight novels, including her most recent YA novel *Snow Apples*, which was nominated for a Governor General's Literary Award. At 83 she is living proof of lifelong learning; she is currently a fourth year student at UBC, majoring in English literature.